THE FLASK

First published in hardback in Great Britain by HarperCollins Children's Books in 2012
First published in paperback in Great Britain by HarperCollins Children's Books in 2012
HarperCollins Children's Books is a division of HarperCollinsPublishers Ltd,
77-85 Fulham Palace Road, Hammersmith, London W6 8JB

The HarperCollins website address is
www.harpercollins.co.uk

1

Text copyright © Nicky Singer 2012

The author asserts the moral right to be identified as the author of this work.

ISBN-978 0 00 743878 5

Printed and bound in England by
Clays Ltd, St Ives plc

MIX
Paper from
responsible sources
FSC® C007454

THE FLASK

NICKY SINGER

HarperCollins *Children's Books*

Also by Nicky Singer

Feather Boy

For older readers

Doll

The Innocent's Story

GemX

Knight Crew

For my daughter Molly,
who taught me everything I needed to know to write this book,
and who is teaching me still.

1

I find the flask the day the twins are born, so I think of these things as joined, as the twins are joined.

The flask is in the desk, though it is hidden at first, just as the desk itself is hidden, shrouded inside the word *bureau* – which is what my gran calls this lump of furniture that arrives in my room. I hate the desk. I hate the bureau. It is a solid, everyday reminder that my aunt Edie is dead.

Aunt Edie isn't – wasn't – my real aunt, she was my great-aunt, so of course she must have been old.

"Ancient," says my friend Zoe. "Over sixty."

Old and small and wrinkled, with skin as dry as paper.

No.

Her bright blue eyes gone milky with age.

No. No!

My aunt Edie blazed.

At the bottom of her garden there was a rockery in which she grew those tiny flowers that keep themselves closed up tight, refusing to unfurl until the sun comes out. They could be closed up for hours, for days, and then suddenly burst into life, showing their dark little hearts and their delicate white petals with the vivid pink tips. That's what I sometimes thought about Aunt Edie and me. That I was the plant all curled up and she was the blazing sun. That she, and only she, could open up my secret heart.

A week after her death, I find myself standing by that rockery staring at the bare earth.

"Looking for the mesembryanthemums?" says Si. Si's my stepfather and he's good with long words.

I say nothing.

"They're annuals, those flowers, the ones you used to like. Don't think she had the chance to plant any this year."

I say nothing.

"What're you thinking, Jess?"

Si is good with questions. He's good with answers. He's good at talking. He's been talking in my life since I was two.

"About the music," I say.

I'm thinking about Aunt Edie and the piano in her drawing room. About how her tiny hands used to fly over the keys and the room fill with the sound of her music and her laughter. I'm thinking about the very first time she lifted me on to the stool to sit beside her as she played. I must have been about three years old. There was no music on the stand in front of her, she played, as she always did, from memory, or she just made stuff up. But I didn't know that then. I thought the music was in her hands. I thought music flowed out of people's fingers.

"Come on, Jess, your turn now!"

And that very first day, she put my hands next to hers. My hands on the keys of the piano, the keys to a new universe. And, of course, I can't have made a tune, I must have crashed and banged, but that's not how I remember it. I remember that she could make my fingers flow with music too. I remember my dark little heart opening out.

After that I couldn't climb on to that stool fast enough. Every time I went to her house, I would pull her to the piano and she would lift me, laughing. When I sat on that stool nothing else in the world existed. Just me and Edie and the music. Time passed and my legs got longer. I didn't need to be lifted on to the stool. And still we played. Hidden little me – unfurling.

"Where shall we go, Jess?" she'd ask "What's your song today?"

My song.

Our song.

I thought it would last for ever.

Then she was dead. It was Gran who found her. Gran and Aunt Edie were sisters. They had keys to each other's houses, had lived next door to each other for the best of forever. In the fence that separates their gardens there is a little gate. During daylight hours, summer and winter, they kept their back doors open, and you never knew, if you called on them, in whose house you'd find them. So they were joined too.

All sorts of things I'd thought of as separate before the twins were born turn out to be joined.

2

The whole family gathers at the crematorium for the funeral. The hearse is late. My cousin Alistair, who is only five, keeps asking when Aunt Edie is going to arrive. Finally, the hearse turns up with the great brass-handled coffin.

"But where's Aunt Edie?" persists Alistair.

The grown-ups hush him, but I know what he means. You're invited to Aunt Edie's for tea and there she is with a plate of Marmite sandwiches. You're invited to her funeral, why wouldn't she be there too? Aunt Edie at the crematorium with a plate of Marmite sandwiches.

Besides, as I know (and Alistair obviously knows), you can't put the sun in a box.

After the service there is a party at Gran's which

Si calls a *wake*. I don't ask about the word *wake* but Si, with his Best Explaining Voice, tells me anyway. The old English root of the word, which means *being awake*, he says, changed in late medieval times to *wacu*. He pronounces this like *wacko*. It means *watching over someone*, he tells me. People used to sit up overnight, apparently, with dead bodies, watching.

I wacu the wacko people at the wacu. There are some I don't know and no one else seems to know them either as they are standing in a corner by themselves. Mum is sitting on the window seat, weighed down by the coming birth. I listen to her hiccup, she can barely breathe because of the two babies pressed together inside her. She asks me to take some sandwiches to the newcomers. There's one plate of Marmite so I take that. The strangers – two men and a woman – don't notice me at first because they are deep in conversation. They're talking about Aunt Edie's money and about who is going to get it as she doesn't have any children of her own and therefore no grandchildren.

"Sandwich?" I say.

"Oh – and who do we have here?" says the woman, as though I just morphed into a three-year-old.

"Jessica," I say. No one calls me Jessica unless they're

angry with me. But I don't like this woman with her hard face and very pink lipstick and I don't want her to call me Jess, which is what the people I love call me.

"And what's in the sandwiches, Jessica?"

"Marmite."

"Oh – not for me, thanks."

"It was Aunt Edie's favourite," I say.

"Why don't you have one then, Jessica?" the woman says.

I have three. I stand there munching them in front of those strangers even though I'm not in the least hungry. When I've finished I say, "Aunt Edie left everything to Gran."

Si told me that too.

Si doesn't believe in keeping things from children.

3

Later Gran says, "I want to give you something, Jess; something of Edie's." She pauses. "Edie would have wanted that. What would you like, Jess?"

I do not say the desk.

I certainly do not say the bureau.

I say, "The piano."

This cannot be a surprise to my grandmother, but her hand flies to her mouth as if, instead of saying the piano, I'd said the moon.

"I don't know," says Gran from behind her hand. "I don't know about that. I mean, I'll have to talk it over with your mum. And Si."

Mum says, "You already have a piano, Jess."

This is true and not true. There is a piano in our house, an old upright, offered – free of charge – to anyone who cared to remove it when the Tinkerbell Nursery closed down when I was about six. I jumped at the chance of a piano — any piano. But the keys of the Tinkerbell piano were hit for too long by too many small fingers with no music in them at all. The felt of the piano's hammers is worn and the C above middle C always sticks and the top A doesn't sound at all, no matter what the piano tuner does.

Aunt Edie's piano has a full set of working notes. Aunt Edie's piano keeps its pitch even though it's only tuned once a year. Aunt Edie's piano holds all the songs we ever made together.

It's also a concert grand.

Si says, "This is a small house, Jess."

This is also true and not true. The house is small, but the garage is huge.

Si says, "You can't keep a piano in a garage, Jessica."

And you can't. Not when the garage is full up with bits and pieces for your stepfather's Morris 1000 Traveller. And the Traveller itself. And the *donor* cars he keeps for spare parts.

"What about the bureau?" says Gran.

"Bureau?" I say.

"Desk," says Si. "A desk's a great idea. A girl your age

can't be doing her homework at the kitchen table for ever."

"It belonged to my father, Jess," says Gran. "Your great-grandfather."

But I never met my great-grandfather. I don't care about him, and I don't care about his desk.

But it still arrives.

That's when I learn you don't always get what you want in life, you get what you're given.

Which is how it is for the twins.

4

It is as if the desk has landed from space. My room is small and it has small and mainly modern things in it. A single bed with a white wooden headboard and a white duvet stitched with yellow daisies, a chrome-and-glass computer station, a mirror in a silver frame, a slim chest of drawers. And a small(ish) space, where they put the desk.

Two men puff and heave it up the stairs. They are narrow stairs. They bang it into the doorjamb getting it into the room and then they plonk it down in the space and push it hard against the wall.

"Don't make them like they used to," says the sweatier of the two men. "Thank the Lord."

The desk – the bureau – is made of dark wood. It has four drawers with heavy brass locks and heavy brass handles, which make me think of Aunt Edie's coffin. The desk bit is a flap. You pull out two runners, either side of the top drawer, and fold the desk down to rest on them. One of the runners, the one on the left, is wobbly, and if you're not careful, it just falls out on the floor. Or your foot.

Si comes for an inspection. "I could probably fix that runner," he says. "Or you could just be careful. It's not difficult. Look."

I look.

"Marvellous," Si says, testing the flap. "You can do your homework and then – Bob's your uncle – fold it all away."

"I hate it," I say.

"It's a desk," says Si. "Nobody hates a desk."

5

The desk squats in my room. I don't touch it, I don't put anything in it, I don't even look at it more than I can help, but it certainly looks at me; it scowls and glowers and mocks me.

Here I am, it says. *Just what you wanted, right? A bureau.*

I turn my back on that bureau. But it still stares at me – stares and stares out of the mirror.

I turn the mirror to face the wall.

Some weeks later, I hear Mum puffing upstairs. She puffs more than the removal men, because of carrying the weight of the babies all curled together inside her. And also the weight of the worry they are causing.

"Jess," she says, stopping by my door.

"Yes?"

"Jess – I wish you could have had the piano too."

And that makes me want to cry, the way things do when you think nobody understands but actually they do.

6

The next day my friend Zoe comes round.

Zoe is a dancer. She doesn't have the body of a dancer; she's not slim and poised. In fact she's quite big, big-boned, and increasingly, curvy. But when she dances you think it is what she was born to do. I love watching Zoe dance. When Zoe dances she's like me with the piano – nothing else exists, she loses herself in it.

Otherwise, we're not really very alike at all. She's loud and I'm quiet. She's funny and I'm not. And she likes boys. Mum says that it's because, even though we're in the same year at school, she's the best part of twelve months older than me and it makes a difference. Mum says it's also to do with the fact that she's the youngest child in their family.

Soon I will not be the youngest child in our family.

I will no longer be an only child.

Si says, "Girls grow up too fast these days."

And I don't ask him what he means by this or whether he'd prefer Zoe (I've a feeling he doesn't like Zoe that much) to go back to wearing a Babygro, because this will only start A Discussion.

I have other friends of course — Em, Alice — but it's Zoe I see most often, not least because she lives at the bottom of our cul-de-sac, so she just waltzes up and knocks on our door.

Like today.

Then she pounds up the stairs and bursts into my room. Sometimes I think I'll ask her if it's possible for her to come into a room so quietly no one would notice her, which is something I'm quite good at. But I'm not sure she'd understand the task, which is another reason why I like her.

"Hi, hi, hi. Hi!" says Zoe. She wheels about, or tries to, which is when she comes face to face with the desk.

"What," she says, "is that?!"

"It's a bureau," I say.

"A what?"

"A bureau."

"But what's it doing here?"

"It belonged to my aunt Edie."

"It's hideous," she says. "And ancient."

Ancient is one of her favourite words. Anything more than two weeks old is ancient as far as Zoe is concerned.

"It's George III," I say. Si again.

"Hideous, ancient and *pre-owned*. Who'd want something that already belonged to some George whatever?" she says.

I'm going to explain that George Whatever didn't own this piece of furniture, that he just happened to be on the throne of England when it was made, but that would turn me into Si, so I don't.

"Hideous, ancient, pre-owned and bashed up," she continues.

Bashed up?

I actually take a look at the desk. It's not bashed up. And the wood isn't as dark as I'd thought either, in fact it's a pale honey colour, and the grain is quite clear so, even though it's over two hundred and fifty years old you can still imagine the tree from which it was originally cut. There are dents in the surface of course and scratches too, but it doesn't look bashed up, just as though it has lived a little, lived and survived.

"It's not bashed up," I say.

"What?"

"And it's not hideous. Look at the locks," I say. "Look at the handles."

The locks and the handles are also not as I'd thought. They're not heavy, not funereal, in fact they're quite delicate. Around the keyholes are beautiful little curls of brass in the shape of leaves and even the little brass-headed nails that hold the handles in place are carefully banged in to just look like part of the pattern.

"Hideous, ancient, pre-owned and IN THE WAY," says Zoe. She pirouettes. "I mean, how is a person to dance in this room any more?"

Then she sees the mirror turned against the wall.

"And what's this?" she says. "Are you having a bad face day?"

She hangs the mirror the correct way round and checks to see if she has any spots, which of course she doesn't. Even when she gets to be a proper teenager I doubt if she'll have spots. Things like that don't happen to Zoe.

"I'm sorry about the dancing, Zo," I say. "But I really like this bureau. In fact," I add, experimenting, "I think I love it."

"Huh?" says Zoe, who's still searching for spots.

Sometimes I think Zoe is a mirror. I look into her to find out who I really am.

7

As soon as Zoe leaves (flamboyant twirl and a shout of
Bye-eee as she flies down the stairs), I take my chair and
sit at the desk.

I never saw Aunt Edie at this desk, as I saw her so
often at the piano. But she must have sat here, I realise.
Sat writing letters, private things, not things you do
when you have guests in the house. I pull out the
runners (and Si is right about this, it isn't difficult at
all) and lay down the lid.

Inside it is like a little castle. In the middle, there is
a small arched doorway, the door itself hinged between
two tiny carved wooden pillars. On either side of the
door are stepped shelves and cubbyholes of different
sizes, to store envelopes or paper, I suppose. There are
also four drawers, two wide shallow ones next to the

pillars, and at either edge of the desk two narrower, longer ones. The desktop itself slides away if you pull a little leather tab. Underneath is a cavernous little underdrawer.

"That's where they would have kept the inkwells," says Si in passing.

I can see dark stains which could have been ink. People writing at this desk long before Aunt Edie. I imagine a quill pen scratching out a love letter. And suddenly those faraway people who sat at this desk, family or strangers, they don't seem so faraway at all. They seem joined to me by the desk and all the things that have been written and thought here. And then I think about Edie herself, and how maybe she loved this desk. Sun-bright Edie, maybe coming here to be quiet, to be still, to unfurl her own dark heart.

Then I know I want to claim this desk after all.

8

But I still don't put anything in the desk. Not until the morning my mother is to deliver the babies. This is going to be a long day, a difficult day. "We'll need to keep busy," Gran says; "you and me."

Gran has agreed to stay in the house with me so that Si can be in the operating theatre with Mum.

"It's an elective caesarean, Jess," says Si. "The operation itself is quite safe."

They have to go in the night before, as Mum is first on the list. Si stands in the hall holding Mum's suitcase.

"Don't worry, Jess," Mum says, and stretches out her arms for me. But I can't get close, because of the babies. "I'll bring them home safe," she whispers into my hair. "I will."

"Time to go," says Si.

I lie awake a long time that night. Keeping vigil. Watching. I imagine Mum being awake. And Si. And probably the babies too, waiting.

In the morning I skip breakfast.

"You're growing," said Gran. "You have to eat."

But I can't.

I go to my room and start on the desk. I have decided that I will put in some homework stuff, but also some private things. In one of the cubbyholes I lodge my English dictionary, my French dictionary, my class reader. I pay attention to the height of the books, their colour, shuffling them about until I am sure that I have the correct book (the stubby French dictionary), in the middle. In the inkwell space, I put pens, pencils, glue, sticky tape and my panda rubber with the eyes fallen off.

Then I move on to more precious things. Behind the little arched door, I put ScatCat. He's a threadbare grey, his fur worn thin from having slept in my arms every night for the first four years of my life. His jet-black eyes are deep and full of memories. I think I'd still be sleeping with him if Spike hadn't arrived. More about Spike later. To keep Scat company, I add the family of green glass cats made as I watched by a glassmaker one summer holiday. Then I add a bracelet that Zoe made for me (plaited strands of pink and purple thread) and also one made by another good friend – Em – (purple and green) when we were in year 5. I once suggested we make a thread friendship bracelet for the three of us, winding Zoe's colours and Em's and mine (purple and blue) all together. Zoe laughed at me. She said friendship bracelets could only be exchanged one-to-one. That's what Best Friends meant, Zoe said. Didn't I understand about Best Friends? I close the little arched door.

Next I select my father's ivory slide rule. Not Si's slide rule, but one which belonged to my real father. Gran thrust it into my hand one day.

"Here," she said, quite roughly. "Your father had this when he was about your age. You should have it now."

"What is it?" I asked.

"A slide rule, of course."

I must have looked puzzled.

"It was how people did maths," said Gran. "Before calculators."

Before calculators sounded a bit like *Before the Ark*. It made my father seem further away not nearer. Or it did until I held the slide rule. Carefully crafted in wood, overlaid with ivory ("I know we shouldn't really trade ivory," said Gran, "but this elephant has been dead a long, long while"), it's bigger and deeper than a normal ruler with a closely fitting sliding section in the middle slightly broader than a pencil. Along all its edges carved numbers are inked in black.

"It originally belonged to your grandfather. Passed down," Gran said. She paused. "Useless now, I suppose. It's useless, isn't it?"

Gran talks to me quite often about my father, although only when we are alone. Normally it makes me uncomfortable, not because I'm not interested, but because she always seems to require a response from me and I'm never quite sure what that response should be. And the more she looks at me, the more she wants, the less I seem to be able to give. Though I think she believes that, if she talks about him enough, I'll remember him. It will unlock memories of my own. But I was only nine months old when he died and I remember nothing.

But the slide rule is different. It's the first thing I've ever held in my hands that he held in his.

"It's not useless," I say. "I like it. Thank you."

And all the roughness falls away from her.

I'm thinking all this as I select a drawer for my father's ivory slide rule. Right or left? I choose the right, slip it in. Then I change my mind.

I just change my mind.

I open the left drawer and transfer the slide rule. But it won't go, it won't fit. I push at it, feel the weight of its resistance. I push harder, the drawers are an equal pair, so what fits in one has to fit in the other.

Only it doesn't.

I pull out the right-hand drawer. It runs the full depth of the desk, plenty long enough for the slide rule. I pull out the left-hand drawer. It is less than half the length of its twin. Yet it isn't broken. It is as perfectly formed as on the day it was made.

Which is when I put my hand into the dark, secret space that lies behind that drawer.

And find the flask.

9

My heart gives a little thump. I've no idea, this first time, what I'm touching, except that it is cold and rounded and about the size of my hand. As I draw it out into the light, I feel how neatly its hard, shallow curves fit into my palm.

I call it a flask, but perhaps it is really a bottle, a flattish, rounded glass bottle with a cork in. It is very plain, very ordinary and yet it is like nothing I've ever seen before. The glass is clear – and not clear. There are bubbles in it, like seeds, or tiny silver fish, swimming. And the surface has strange whorls on it, like fingerprints or the shapes of contour lines on a map where there are mountains. I think I should be able to see inside, but I can't quite, because the glass seems to shift and change depending on how the light falls on it: now milky as a pearl; now flashing a million iridescent colours.

I sit and gaze at it for a long while, turning it over and over in my hands, watching its restless colours and patterns. It is a beautiful thing. I wonder how it came into being, who made it? It can't have been made by machine, it is too special, too individual. I remember the glassmaker who made my green cats and I imagine a similar man in a leather apron blowing life down a long tube into this glass, putting his own breath into it, lung to lung, pleased when the little vessel expanded. And then, as I keep on looking, the contours don't look like contours any more but ribs, and the bowl of glass a tiny ribcage.

I have these thoughts because of the babies. Everything in the last nine months has been about the babies. They get into and under everything. They aren't even born and they can make you frightened, they can make Mum cry, they can make me see things that aren't there under shifting glass. Because, all of a sudden, I think I can see something beneath the surface of the glass after all.

Something and nothing.

I do make things up. Si says, "You are certainly not a scientist, Jessica. Scientists look at the evidence and then they come to a view." But it's not just Si, it's Gran and even Mum. They say I make things up. I see things that aren't there. And hear them sometimes too. Like now, beneath the glass, through the glass.

Some movement, a blink, a sigh. A song. Some sadness.

The sensation of life, of a ribcage, breathing.

"Jessica!" That's a shout, a real-world shout. Gran is shouting. "Jessica, Jess!"

I jolt out of myself. "What?"

"The phone, Jess."

Gran is standing at the bottom of the stairs, the phone in her hand.

It has come. The message. She knows. She knows about the babies.

I abandon everything, fly down the stairs, rip the phone from her.

"Yes?"

It is Si.

"Jess," he says. "Jess."

"Yes!"

"They're alive. They're alive, Jess." His voice doesn't sound like his normal voice, it sounds floating. I conjure his face. His eyes are full of stars.

I know I'm supposed to say something , but I don't know what.

"Isn't it wonderful?" says Gran.

"And they both have a heart," says Si. "Two hearts, Jess. One heart each."

Then I find something to say.

"Omphalopagus," I say.

10

Omphalopagus is the technical term for babies joined at the lower chest. These type of babies never share a heart, so I don't know why Si is so surprised. After all, it was Si who did the research, hours and hours of it on the net. Si who taught me the word, made me pronounce it back to him. *Omphalo* – umbilicus. *Pagus* – fastened, fixed. Fixed at the navel. The twins umbilically joined to each other and to Mum and right back through history to the Greeks who coined the word in the first place.

Me and the joins.

Si and the statistics.

Si's endless statistics. Seventy per cent of conjoined twins are girls. Thirty-nine per cent are stillborn. Thirty-four per cent don't make it through the first day of life.

Si's eyes, shining.

"Can you give me back to Gran now, Jess," says Si.

As I hand over the phone, I remember the night of Mum's nineteen-week scan. I'd come down for a raid on the cereal cupboard. Si and Mum were talking in the sitting room, hushed, serious talk.

"They're gifts of God," I heard Mum say.

I stood at the door of the kitchen waiting for Si to put Mum right about that. I waited for him to tell Mum what he'd told me earlier that afternoon that, despite a great deal of mystical mumbo jumbo talked about conjoined twins down the ages, they are actually just biological lapses, slips of nature. Embryos that begin to divide into identical twins, but never complete the process, or split embryos that somehow fuse back together again. A small error, a malfunction, nothing to be surprised about, considering the cellular complexity of a human being.

I wait for him to say this. But he doesn't.

"They're miracles," Mum says. "Our miracles. And I don't care what anyone says. They're here to stay."

And Si doesn't go on to mention the thirty-nine per cent of conjoined twins who don't make it through the birth canal, or the thirty-four per cent who die on day one.

He just takes her in his arms and lets her bury her head in his chest. I see them joined there. Head to chest.

11

I've only been gone from my bedroom a matter of minutes, but it feels like a lifetime. Even the room doesn't look the way it did before. It's bigger, brighter, there is sunlight splashing through the window.

"The babies," I shout. "They're alive!" I jump on the bed and throw myself into a wild version of a tribal dance Zoe once taught me. Then I catch sight of myself in the mirror and stop. Immediately.

I also see, in the mirror, the flask. It has fallen over, it's lying on its side on the desk.

No. No!

I scoot off the bed.

Please don't be cracked, please don't be broken.

The flask has only just entered my life and yet, I realise suddenly, I feel very powerfully about it.

Connected, even. I find myself lurching forwards, grabbing for it. But it isn't my beautiful, breathing flask, it is just a bottle. Something you might dig up in any old back garden. It isn't broken, but it might just as well be, because the colours are gone and so are the patterns. No, that's not true, there are whorls on the surface of the glass still, but they aren't moving any more, and the bubbles, my little seed fish, they aren't swimming. And there is nothing − *nothing* − inside.

I feel a kind of fury, as though somebody has given me something very precious and then just snatched it away again. I realise I already had plans for that flask. I was going to remove the cork and...

The cork − where is the cork?

It isn't in the bottle. I scan the desk. It isn't on the desk. But how can it be anywhere but in the bottle or on the desk? Did I imagine a cork? No, I saw it: a hard, discoloured thing, lodged in the throat of the flask. I look into the empty bottle, as if the cork might just miraculously appear. But it doesn't. The smell of the bottle is of cold and dust. There can't have been anything in that bottle.

And yet there was.

There was something crouched inside that glass, waiting.

No, not crouched, that makes it sound like an animal. And the thing didn't have that sort of form, it was just something moving, stirring. Then I see it, the cork. Look! There on the floor. It's not close to the flask, not just fallen out and lying on the desk, but a full metre away. Maybe more. To carry the cork that far something big, something powerful, must have come out of the flask, burst from it.

So where is that thing now?

12

It's on the window sill.

What I thought was a patch of sunlight isn't sunlight at all. It's bright like sunlight, but it doesn't fall right, doesn't cast the right shadows. Light coming through a windowpane starts at the sun and travels for millions of miles in dead straight lines. You learn that in year 6. Light from the sun is not curved, or lit from inside, or suddenly iridescent as a soap bubble or milky as a pearl. It doesn't expand and pulse and move. It doesn't breathe. Whatever is on the window sill, it isn't light from the sun.

I go towards it. It would be a lie to say I'm not frightened. I am frightened, terrified even, but I'm also drawn. I can't help myself. I remember my old maths teacher, Mr Brand, breaking off from equations one day and going to stand at the window where there was a slanted sunbeam. He cupped his hands in the beam and looked at the light he held – and didn't hold.

"You can't have it," he said. "You can't ever have it."

And all of the class laughed at him. Except me. I knew what he meant because I've tried to capture sunbeams too.

And now I want the thing on the window sill, because it is strange and beautiful and I don't want to lose it again. I don't want to feel what I felt when I saw that the flask was empty, which is sick and hollow, my stomach clutching just like in the moment when Mum told me Aunt Edie was dead.

So I move very slowly and quietly, as though the thing is an animal after all and might take fright. And it does seem to be vibrating – or trembling, I can't tell which – as though it is aware of me, watching me, though something without eyes cannot watch.

"It's all right," I find myself saying. "It's all right. I won't hurt you."

I won't hurt it! What about it hurting me?

My room's not big, as I've said, but it takes an age to cross. I am just a hand-stretch away from the pearly, pulsing light when there is a sudden whoosh, like a wind got up from nowhere, and I feel a rush and panic, but I don't know if it is my rush and panic or that of the thing which seems to whip and curl past my head and pour itself back into the flask.

Back into the flask!

Quick as a flash, I put my thumb over the opening and I hold it down tight as I scrabble in the desk for my sticky tape. I pull at the tape, bite some off, jam it over the open throat of the flask and then wind it again and again around the neck, so the thing cannot escape.

I have it captured.

Captured!

Then I feel like one of those boys you read about in books that pull the wings off flies: violent, cruel. But here's the question: if you had something in your bedroom that flew and breathed and didn't obey the laws of science, would you want it at liberty?

There you are then.

13

When my heart calms down, I feel I owe the flask (or the thing inside it) an explanation. I think I should tell the truth, about the fear as well as the excitement. But I don't know who or what I'm dealing with, so I also feel I shouldn't give too much away. I should be cautious. Si's always saying that: a man of science proceeds with care. Or *If you're going to mix chemicals, Jess, put your goggles on.*

I'm not sure what sort of goggles I need to deal with the thing in the flask, but I think the least I can try is an apology.

"I'm sorry about the sticky tape," I say.

I'm not really expecting a reply and I don't get one, but the movement inside the flask does seem to become a little less frantic, so I have the feeling the thing is listening.

"I guess you must have been in that flask a long time," I say next.

Where does that remark come from? From the cold and the dust I smelt in the bottle? Or from some story-book knowledge of things in bottles, genies in lamps? What am I imagining, that the thing is some trapped spirit cursed to remain in the flask for a thousand years until – until what? Until Jessica Walton arrives with her father's ill-fitting slide rule? They say (correction: Si says) if you put a sane person in a lunatic asylum for any length of time they become as mad as the inmates. Me? I'm talking to a thing in a flask.

I'm calling it *you*.

The word *you* implies that the thing I'm talking to is alive. I mean you don't say *you* to a box of tissues, do you? Or to a hairbrush or a necklace or a mobile phone. So I am making a definite assumption about the thing being alive. Mr Pugh, our biology teacher, says that only things that carry out all seven of the life processes can be said to be alive. Pug calls this Mrs Nerg.

M – for movement

R – for reproduction

S – for sensitivity

N – for nutrition

E – for excretion

R – for respiration

G – for growth

I look at the thing in the flask. Movement – no doubt about that. Reproduction. I'm not sure I want to think about that right now. Sensitivity. Definitely. It's sensitive to me, I'm sensitive to it. Nutrition. Does the thing eat? Unlikely. It doesn't have a mouth. But then plants eat and they don't have mouths. Excretion. Not important. If you don't eat you don't need to excrete. Respiration. Yes, it breathes, doesn't it? And it has to get energy from somewhere or it couldn't move and it certainly moves. Growth. Yes again; I think I can imagine it growing.

To be alive, Pug says, you have to be able to carry out all seven of the processes. Not two, or five or one. All seven.

I think Pug may have missed out on some of his training. This thing is definitely alive.

"Who are you?" I say. "What are you?"

The thing does not respond.

I retreat a bit. "I think you'll be safer in the flask for a while," I say.

I mean, of course, that I'll feel safer if the thing is in the flask. I've heard adults do this. They tell you something they want by making it sound useful to you, like, *You'll be much warmer in your coat, won't you?*

"Because," I add, "I have to go to the hospital in a minute. Gran's taking me to the hospital."

No reply.

"To see the babies."

No reply.

"So I'm just going to pop you (*you*) back in the desk for a bit."

No reply.

"OK?"

"You see, I noticed how you rushed back in the flask yourself, so it must be your home, I guess. Am I right?"

No reply.

"My name's Jess, by the way."

Some little silver seed fish, swimming.

"How do you do that? How do you make the fish swim?"

No reply.

"It's beautiful."

No reply.

"So just wait, OK?"

No reply.

"Promise?"

Very gently, I place the flask back into the dark space behind the left-hand drawer in the desk.

"See you later," I say, as I leave the room.

14

Our local hospital is too small to deal with cases like the twins', so we have to go to the city. It's a long drive.

"Your mum will be very tired, you know that, don't you?" Gran says.

She makes it sound like we shouldn't be going, but I know why we're going. In case the twins belong in the thirty-four per cent who die on day one.

The Special Care Baby Unit is in the tower-block part of the hospital, on the fifteenth floor. We come out of the lift to face a message to tell us we are *In the Zone* and to make sure we scrub ourselves with the Hygienic Hand Rub. The doors to the unit are locked and we have to ring to gain admission.

Si hears us as we check in at the nurses' station

and comes out to greet us.

"Angela," he says to Gran and then, "Jess." And he puts his hand out to touch me, which he doesn't usually. I look at his eyes. They aren't sparkling, but they are smiling. "Come on in."

There are four incubators in the room and five nurses. Two of the nurses are wearing flimsy pink disposable aprons and throwing things into bins. There's an air of serious hush, broken only by the steady blip of ventilators. Beside each cot is a screen with wavy lines of electronic blue, green and yellow. I don't know what they measure, but they're the sort of machines you see in films that go into a single flat line when people die. Mum is not sitting or standing, but lying on a bed. They must have wheeled her in on that bed, and braked her up next to the twins. She doesn't look up immediately when we come into the room; all her focus, all her attention is on my brothers.

Brothers.

All through the pregnancy, Mum's been calling them my brothers. When the twins are born, when your brothers are born... But, I realise, standing in the hospital Special Care Unit, that they are not my brothers. Not full brothers, anyway. We share a mother, but not a father, so they are my half-brothers. But half-brothers sounds as if they're only half here or as if they don't quite belong. And that's scary. Or maybe it's actually me that doesn't quite belong any more, as though a chunk of what I thought of as family has somehow slid away. And that's even scarier.

So, I'm going to call them brothers – my brothers.

Mum looks up, shifts herself up on her pillows a little when she sees me, although I can see it hurts her.

"Jess… come here, love."

I come and she puts her arms right around me, even though it's difficult with leaning from the bed.

"Look." She nods towards the incubator. "Here they are, here they are at last."

They lie facing each other, little white knitted hats on their heads, hands entwined. Yes, they're holding hands. Fast asleep and tucked in under a single white blanket they look innocent. Normal.

"Aren't they beautiful?" says Mum.

"Yes," I say. And it's true, though there is something frail about them, two little birds who can't fly and are lucky to have fallen together in such a nest.

"You were a beautiful baby too, Jess."

She is making it ordinary, but it isn't ordinary.

Somewhere beneath that blanket, my brothers are joined together and I want to see that join. At least I do now, although for months the idea of the join has been making me feel queasy.

There, I've said it.

The truth is, when Mum first told me she was pregnant I felt all rushing and hot. Not about the join, which we didn't know about then, or even about them being twins. No, I felt rushing and hot about her being pregnant at all. I can't really explain it except to say I didn't want people looking at my mother, I didn't want them watching her swelling up with Si's baby. It seemed to be making something very private go very public. And I didn't like myself for the way I felt, so when it turned out to be twins, and conjoined twins at that, I hid myself in the join. I made this the secret. I didn't want people to know about the join (I told Zoe, I told Em), because of all the mumbo jumbo talked about such twins down the centuries. I didn't tell them that I wasn't so sure about the babies myself, that the idea of the join actually made me feel sick to my stomach. I kept very quiet about that.

Am I a bad person?

A nurse is hovering and sees the babies stir.

"Do you want to hold them, Mum?" the nurse says as if my mother is her mother.

"Yes," says Mum.

Si helps Mum into a comfortable sitting position while the nurse unhitches one side of the incubator and adjusts some tubes. Then he stands protectively as the nurse puts a broad arm under both babies and draws them out. Si never takes his eyes off the babies and there is something fierce in his gaze and something soft too, that I've never seen before.

"There now," says the nurse as she gives the babies to Mum. They are in Mum's arms, but they are still facing each other, of course. The nurse has been careful to keep the blanket round the babies as she lifts them and she's careful now to tuck it in.

One of the babies makes a little yelping noise and Mum puts a finger to the baby's lips and he appears to suck.

"They're doing very well," says Mum, and then she loosens the blanket.

The babies are naked, naked except for two outsized nappies which seem to go from their knees to their waists – where the join begins. Mum leaves the blanket open quite deliberately. Gran turns her head away, but

I look. I look long and hard as Mum means me to do.

The babies' skin is a kind of brick colour, as if their blood is very close to the surface, and it is also dry and wrinkled, as if they are very old rather than very young. Aunt Edie again. But the skin where they join is smooth and actually rather beautiful, like the webs between your fingers. It makes me feel like crying.

Very gently, Mum strokes the place where her children join, and then she draws the blanket back around them.

I realise then I don't know what the babies are called.

"Richie," says Mum, "after Si's father. And Clem, after mine."

15

It seems to be enough for Mum. She lies back and closes her eyes and the nurse comes and takes the babies away again. I think Si would like to lift them himself, but he doesn't dare. Maybe he feels they are too fragile, that he'd hurt them.

Mum seems to have gone into an almost immediate sleep, and just for a moment, I feel we might all be just some dream of hers – me and Si and Gran and the babies all rather unlikely conjurings of her exhausted brain. And then, as I watch her chest rise and fall, I think about the flask and that seems like an even deeper dream. I had been going to tell Mum about the flask, how I found it in the desk and how it was full of something unearthly, something beautiful and scary at the same time and how I captured it, because I feel

fierce and soft towards it, just like Si does towards the
twins, but that I also feel bad because, as Mr Brand says,
you can't catch things that are supposed to be wild and
free and…

"I think we ought to go now," says Gran.

"Mum…" I say.

"Ssh," says Si. "She needs to rest."

16

By the time we get back home it is almost dark.

"Who's that?" Gran asks as we turn into our drive.

It's Zoe, of course, knocking at our front door. She turns as she hears the car pull up. I wind down my window.

"Want to come to the park?" she asks.

Zoe and I often go to the park at dusk. It's one of our little rituals. We swing on the swings after all the little kids have gone home. We swing and talk. Or Zoe dances. She dances around the swan on its large metal spring. She dances along the wooden logs which are held up by chains, she backflips off the slide. When she's tired, which isn't often, we lie together on our backs in the half-moon swing and look at the sky. Or I look at the sky anyway. She looks upwards, but what she sees I don't know, because people can look in the same place but not see the same things, can't they?

"Bit late for the park," says Gran.

But I want to go to the park because I want some private time with Zoe. I want to tell her how beautiful my brothers are, after all; I want to take time, sharing all the details of those little birds and the web of their join. I want to look in her eyes, see myself reflected in the mirror of her, the big sister of two baby boys.

"Please," I say to Gran. "Just for half an hour."

I also want to tell Zoe about the flask.

"Well," says Gran. She looks at her watch. "Oh, all right then. Just while I make dinner."

"Thanks, Gran," I say, and I actually lean over and give her a kiss.

Zoe doesn't know we've just come from the hospital and I don't tell her. I want to be lying in the half-moon when I tell her about the babies. I want her to be the first to know, as she was about the join. A special moment, shared. Luckily, as we head down the cul-de-sac, she's already chatting to me, she's telling me about her sister's boyfriend and his new car and how her mother won't let the boyfriend drive Zoe about, but she doesn't mind him driving her sister about, which is ridiculous and...

And soon we're at the park and Paddy and Sam are

there too with a football and two jumpers to mark a goal. Paddy isn't Paddy's real name, his real name is Maxim, but he doesn't look like a Maxim so everyone calls him Paddy. He has a big, round, smiling face and he bounces through life like a beach ball. Happy and full of air. Or at least that's what I think. Zoe thinks he's massively handsome and has An Outstanding Sense of Humour. It's Paddy, in fact, that Zoe has her eyes on.

I'm desperate to skirt behind the conker tree so we can get to the playground unseen, but Zoe is heading straight for the boys.

"Zoe…" I start urgently, clutching at her jacket.

But she's already pulling away, calling. "Hi! Hi! Hi Paddy. Hi Sam."

So there I am, trailing behind her.

The boys look up.

"Hey," Sam says. Sam wears slouchy trousers and likes to think he's cool. "How's it going?"

"Great," says Zoe.

We haven't seen either boy since school broke up for the Easter holidays.

"We were just going to the swings," I say quickly.

"Well, in a mo," says Zoe.

Paddy looks at Zoe and then he looks at me. "Did

the babies arrive yet?" he asks.

And there's a moment where I could just say no, I could just say no and then we could walk away, and I could tell Zoe like I planned to as we lay in the half-moon swing.

"Well, did they?"

"Yes," I say.

"What?" shrieks Zoe.

"They arrived." I think I say it because I don't want to deny them any more, these baby birds who are my brothers. I need them to be around me. Solid.

"Why didn't you tell me?" shrieks Zoe.

Why didn't you ask?

"Oh, right," says Sam, whose interests are pretty much confined to sport and his computer.

"And?" asks Paddy.

"And they're beautiful," I say. "Boys. Two boys."

"They're all right then?" says Zoe. "They're both all right?"

"They've got eight legs," says Paddy.

"What?" says Sam.

"That's what my nan said," Paddy continues. "They could have eight legs."

"Mumbo jumbo," I say, and I shoot a look at Zoe.

"They have four legs."

"Four!" exclaims Paddy.

"Yes," I say. "Two each. Like normal people."

"Oh – normal!" Paddy laughs.

Zoe's shrugging. Zoe's making out that whatever Paddy's saying, it's nothing to do with her.

"What you all on about?" Sam asks.

"Jess's brothers," says Paddy. "They're not just any old twins. They're Siamese."

Sam is doing knee-ups with the ball. "Siamese?" he says.

"Conjoined." I hear my voice going up, I hear myself about to shout. "The correct term is *conjoined twins*. And as for normal, they *are* normal. Considering the cellular complexity of the average human being, that is." *Shut up, Si.* "They're as normal as me. Or you. If you call that normal."

Paddy ignores *normal*. "Point is," he says, "they're joined down the chest."

Sam drops the ball. He drops his jaw. His mouth hangs open. "Man," he says. "Joined down the chest? Wow. Like, you mean, face to face? Like they're facing each other all the time? Jeez."

"If I was stuck on to my brother," says Paddy,

63

going to retrieve the ball, "if he was the first thing I saw when I woke up and the last thing I saw before I went to sleep, that would kill me."

"More likely kill your brother, being stuck to you," I say. Then I round on Zoe. "Come on," I say. "We're going."

But Zoe's feet seem planted in the ground.

"In the old days," says Paddy, "they put Siamese twins in the circus. People paid to see them."

"Conjoined!" I shout.

"You could do that," Paddy continues. "You could bring your brothers in next term and charge a pound a go to look."

"They might not even last that long," I say. Or maybe I don't say it. Maybe it's the silent thing shouting in my head. *They might not even last that long.*

Paddy's big face is shining with excitement. "I'd pay," he says. "I'd pay to look. Wouldn't you, Sam?"

"Yeah," says Sam.

"You could have a different rate depending on whether it was just a look or a touch," Paddy continues.

"Shut up," I say.

"A pound for a look, two pounds for a good look and a fiver for a touch."

"I said SHUT UP."

"We could call it JFS – Jess's Freak Show."

And now everything that's been silent and bottled up comes frothing and boiling over at last and I go right up to him because I'm going to hit him in the stupid, shining face. I draw back my fist and I lash out as hard and fast as I can, but he just catches my wrist.

"Hey," he says. "Hey. What's up with you? It was only a joke. Can't you take a joke now?"

"I hate you," I scream.

But actually it's Zoe I hate.

17

I turn and march away from the park. Of course, Zoe follows me.

"Jess," she says. "Jess, Jess, Jess!" And now it's her turn to clutch me by the sleeve. "Come on!"

I stop, I wheel about. "Come on *what*, exactly?"

"I never told him," she says. "I didn't."

"Oh, right; he just made it up, did he? Thought it up out of his own stupid little brain?"

"I didn't tell him, Jess, I promise, I swear."

I stare at her. Her eyes are all lit up bright, but not like a mirror. I can't see myself in them, in her. "Then who did?"

"I don't know," Zoe exclaims. "Maybe your mum told his mum and she told Paddy."

"Oh, yeah, right."

"Or Em. You didn't just tell me, did you? You pretended you did, but you didn't. You told Em too. So maybe it was Em who told Paddy."

Very clever. And hurtful, because it's true. I did tell Em actually and I did pretend to Zoe that she was the only one who knew. Why did I do that? Because Zoe can be jealous probably. She can go mental just like she did about the friendship bracelet thing in year 5. But Em's away on holiday. Em's not here to defend herself. "Why would Em tell Paddy? She doesn't even like Paddy. No one likes Paddy." I pause. "Except you."

"I still didn't tell him, Jess. I mean – why would I?"

And I can't say it. I can't say, *Because I think you're beginning to like him more than you like me*, because that sounds totally pathetic. So I say, "For a laugh. So you could both have a laugh behind my back about my so-not-normal brothers."

"Jess, you're way over the top. I didn't tell him. I didn't!"

"So why did you let him say all that stuff, all that eight-leg circus-freak stuff?"

"That's just mumbo jumbo, Jess, you said so yourself. You said people would say stuff like that. How's that my fault?"

"You could have spoken up – you could have said something. Anything."

Now she's silent, biting in her lip.

"But you just stood there," I ram it home. "You let him say all of it and you just stood there."

I start walking again now, turning my back on her and walking, walking.

She runs back after me again, but I shake her off.

"I didn't know I had to say anything. Anyway, you were saying stuff," Zoe remarks to my back. "And what does it matter? They're born now. They're OK."

It matters because she promised, because I trusted her. And I need to go on trusting her. Because of the flask. "Who says they're OK?" I say.

"What?"

"The babies – who says they're OK?"

"You did!" says Zoe. "You said it!"

"I said they were beautiful. I didn't say they were OK."

"Well – are they OK?"

I say nothing.

"Well, are they?"

"I'm not telling you," I say. "I'm not telling you anything ever again."

18

I don't say a single thing over dinner. And if Gran notices she doesn't mention it. She probably thinks it's to do with the babies. And she's right. Everything's to do with the babies these days.

Except the flask.

I delay going up to bed, partly because I'm no good at sleeping when I'm angry, and partly because I expect to see little bits of sticky tape on the floor. I mean, something that can blow a cork from a bottle can burst through sticky tape, right?

Wrong.

There is no sticky tape on the floor. The desk is still closed, the drawer inside shut. I reach my hand in and feel the cold, rounded form of the flask.

"I'm back," I say, sliding my fingers up the throat of

the bottle, just to check the sticky tape is really still in place.

It is.

So I draw the flask out into the light. It is blue. Really blue — like a summer sky. Like happiness. Whatever I expected, it wasn't this.

I just stand and stare, trying to work out whether it is the glass or the thing inside that is blue. But I can't separate the two. Nor can I understand why — despite Zoe and Paddy and the park and the mumbo jumbo — just holding it makes me fizz with joy, as though I am holding a tiny, perfect other universe.

"You're extraordinary," I say. "You know that?"

No reply.

But then what would a universe reply? And I remember Si showing me pictures taken by the Hubble Telescope, pillars of dust 57 trillion trillion miles high and some nebula thing called the eye of God because that's what it looked like, some astonishingly beautiful giant eye. And Si was busy explaining about gas and cusp knots and interstellar collisions, and I was just thinking it was all too much and too beautiful to look at even in a newspaper. And here is something even more extraordinary in the palm of my hand.

I don't want to put the flask back in the dark drawer, I want to keep it close by me. So I take it to my bed, and lay it on my pillow as I undress. I don't know how long the blue will last, the blue and the bright happiness inside me. And it's not just the thing about Zoe (why couldn't it have been my mum talking to Paddy's mum?), it's also the first time, I realise, I've felt really happy since we knew about the babies. The babies have shadowed everything for months, the worry of them. Would they be born alive, and if so, would they be able to survive? And now, this glowing blue seems to have the power to push the gloom away. Or maybe it's just that I've seen the babies. Seen them alive with their bright little bird faces.

I get into bed thinking sleep will come with the sweetest of dreams.

19

But sleep doesn't come.

Not quickly.

Not at all.

My mind will not be quiet, it refuses to listen to my happy heart. The flask is tucked beneath my pillow, but my thoughts still toss about in the park (of course my mum didn't talk to Paddy's mum, why would she?). Eventually, my restless anxiety pokes its way under my brothers' sheet at the hospital.

Richie and Clem.

I'm glad the babies have names, it makes them seem less vulnerable somehow, as though they really are here to stay, have personalities all of their own, a right to exist. Richie seems a slightly bigger name to me than Clem, just as Richie himself, I realise as I picture them again in my mind, is the bigger twin. Not by much, of course, but if one twin could be said to be clinging on to the other, then it is Clem who is clinging to Richie. Clem who, if there is to be trouble, is the weaker one.

Thirty-four per cent of conjoined twins don't make it through the first twenty-four hours.

Clem's a strange name, a strange word. It sounds to me like *clam*. Clem the closed-up clam, clinging.

I turn over.

And over.

I feel bad characterising Clem like this, as though naming him as weaker makes him weaker still. They are both strong, I tell myself.

Strong enough to get through this dangerous night. Their first on earth.

I put my hand under my pillow, reaching for the flask as if blue was something you could feel or touch.

Then my thoughts return to Zoe: Em would never betray a secret and I haven't once seen her talking to Paddy. It's Zoe who's always talking to Paddy. Though I can't check, can't be sure, because Em's away on holiday for pretty much the whole Easter break. But it must have been Zoe, confiding in Paddy. Making the join of the twins the butt of Paddy's Outstanding Sense of Humour, which he clearly gets from his nan and her eight legs and… And my thoughts find the twins, sleeping together, breathing together, the little sheet rising and falling around them. And as they breathe, the flask seems to breathe too, inhaling and exhaling beneath my hand. A tiny ribcage. And then things begin to get muddled and I hear a moan of the sort people make when they're dreaming and they want to wake up and they can't. And I don't know if I am really awake, or just dreaming that I am awake, but I do hear the moan get louder, becoming more of a wail, and suddenly I'm sitting bolt upright in bed, my heart pounding.

It makes me gasp how fast my heart is pounding. It's deeply dark, the middle of the night. So I must have slept after all, slept for a long while. I try to calm myself, to try to remember the blue, the overwhelming happiness. But all I hear is the wail, only it isn't a wail any more, it's a howl. Something dark and inhuman is howling from beneath my pillow.

I stumble and fling myself out of that bed. Fear makes many shapes, but this thing has only one shape, the shape of the flask. The same thing that splashed light on my window sill and held a universe of brilliant blue is now pulsing black wolf howls into my night, into my head.

"Stop, stop, stop!" I want to shout, to scream, but the words are stuck in my throat.

There is nothing for it but to reach through the dark, reach under the pillow. I am afraid the flask will be soft under my hand, like a heart, but it is hard and cold, holding its glass shape. I want to smash it. If I smash it the noise will stop, it will have to stop.

I pick up the flask, intending to fling it against the wall, but that's when the howl goes higher and also softer, not so much wolf as wolf cub, and there is suddenly something so terrible and so sad about the noise that I just pull the flask to my chest and hold it there. Then I rock with it, like you'd rock with a baby who was crying and you had nothing to give but the warmth of your own flesh.

Which is when Gran comes into the room.

"Jess?" she says. "Jess, can't you sleep either?"

"No," I cry. "No!"

The spill of light from the hall makes my bedroom bright and ordinary.

"I thought I heard you," Gran says.

"Heard me?"

"Walking about."

"Water," I say. "I need some water."

"You look half-frozen," she replies. "I'll get the water. Come on now, you get back to bed. It's gone two o'clock."

Gratefully, I get back into bed. Under the covers, I look at the flask. It is not a heart, not a ribcage, it isn't pulsing. There is nothing black about it, but nothing blue either. It is calm and hard and glassy, colourless.

As Gran returns with the water, I slip the flask back beneath the pillow.

"He told you they could die on their first night, didn't he?" Gran says.

"Who?" I say, as though I don't quite understand her. Though of course I do.

"Si. He told you the babies could die, didn't he?"

I shrug.

"He's no business saying things like that." She sits down hard on the edge of the bed. "No business at all."

"He only mentioned the statistics…" I begin.

"Statistics," says Gran, "are bosh."

And I know this. I've heard it all my life.

Statistics are bosh.

Statistics are bosh.

Gran says it like a mantra, her own little song.

This is something else Si has told me about. Something

76

he's explained. Si explains everything; Gran explains nothing. You just have to guess what Gran means, you have to look around her corners. "Your grandmother," said Si, "has never trusted statistics since your father died of something people don't normally die of. Hiatus hernia. A million-to-one chance, that's what the doctors told her. So now she doesn't believe in the numbers game."

I should never have mentioned statistics.

"Anyway," Gran continues, "you saw your brothers. Saw them with your own eyes. They're going to be fine. Do you hear me?"

I hear her.

"So you're not to worry. Right?"

She comes to tuck me in like I'm some baby myself. As she fusses about me, I realise that I will always be her baby in a way that my brothers will not. Si is the twins' father, but not mine. So Gran has no blood relationship with the twins. Gran and the babies – they aren't joined at all.

In the last chink of light, before Gran shuts my door, I check the flask. In its whorls, its worlds, there are a couple of bright seed fish swimming.

After that, I sleep.

20

The following morning, the phone rings at 7.36. Nobody rings our house that early.

I arrive in the kitchen to hear Gran say, "Yes, of course I'll tell her, Si."

She puts down the phone. I wait for her to give me the news.

"Morning, Jess," she says. "Breakfast's up." From the oven she takes a steaming plate of bacon and egg and tomatoes and fried bread. The smell of it makes me want to retch.

"What did he say?" I ask. "What's happened?"

"Your mum's fine," says Gran.

"And the babies?"

"They're fine too." But there is something too bright and too quick about the way she says it.

I look at her. "What?"

"What what?" she repeats.

"What did Si say? What did he want you to tell me?"

Gran wipes her hands on her apron. "Your stepfather," she says, "wanted you to know that your mother and your brothers are fine."

I stare at her and I keep on staring. I want the truth.

"Clem…" Gran says finally, lips pressed tight.

"Yes?"

"He took a little dip in the night… but he's absolutely fine now."

A little dip.

I can't imagine Si using these words. Si would use precise medical terms.

"What kind of 'dip'?"

"Oh, I don't know, Jessica. Nobody said it would be plain sailing. The important thing is that he's OK now."

"And when exactly?" I ask.

"When what?" says Gran.

"When did Clem take this little dip?"

"Does it matter?"

I think of that great sobbing howl.

"Yes. It does matter."

"Look, Jess, I know things have been difficult in this

79

house over the last few months. And I know you didn't sleep very well last night. So I'm going to ignore your tone of voice. But you have to trust me and Si and the doctors. And you have to eat your breakfast."

I sit down. I try my bacon, toy with my egg. In the right-hand pocket of my trousers I can feel the weight of the flask. Calm this morning, colourless. But opalescent on the day the twins were born, its cork bursting from its throat, and then black and howling the night that Clem took a dip.

"Do you ever think," I ask Gran, "that things are more…" I want to use the word *joined*, the word that's been stuck in my head for weeks, but I choose to say *connected*. "Do you think things are more connected than they might appear?"

Gran is eating toast. "I'm not sure I understand you, Jess."

"That there are more things on earth than can be explained by – well, science?"

"Are we talking God?" asks Gran.

"No!" Actually, I think we're talking Si; I'm talking about whether there is more in the universe than can be explained by my stepfather.

"Ghosts?" she hazards.

Ghosts. That makes a patter in my heart. When did the flask come into my life? After Aunt Edie died. And where did it come from? Aunt Edie's desk. Ghosts are spirits without bodies. Like the thing in the flask. And they arrive after people die...

"Jessica?"

"No, no!" I don't want a ghost. A ghost is scary.

Scarier than the howls?

Besides – a ghost doesn't make any sense. Not the ghost of Aunt Edie. I'd know that ghost, surely. And it – she – would know me. We'd chat, wouldn't we? *Hi Jess, it's me, Aunt Edie, just came to see how you were getting on with your piano playing.* And in any case, ghosts don't exist, do they? Pug and his Mrs Nerg wouldn't have anything to do with ghosts. Si wouldn't have anything to do with ghosts. But is a ghost any more extraordinary than a disembodied something connected to the twins?

My mind is going round in circles. I blame Zoe. If Zoe and I were on speaking terms I wouldn't be having to share all this with Gran.

"What do you mean then?" Gran asks.

"I was just thinking... last night – I couldn't sleep, you couldn't sleep and Clem – he wasn't well. Maybe we somehow... sensed that?"

"Nice idea," says Gran. "But a bit far-fetched. It's just worry, I'm afraid. Keeps people awake all the time." She gets up to reboil the kettle. "And knowing too much. Sometimes the less you know, the better."

I say nothing. I don't like the dig at Si. *He told you the babies could die, didn't he? Sometimes the less you know the better.* I'm allowed to have a dig at him, but she isn't. Why is that?

"You've always been a sensitive child, Jessica," Gran continues. "And sometimes that's a good thing." She pauses. "And sometimes it's a curse."

"A curse?"

"You imagine things that simply aren't there."

"Last night," I say, suddenly angry, "there was a howl, a terrible, terrible sobbing howl. Didn't you hear it?"

"Jess love, it was a difficult night. You were tossing and turning. I know – I peeked in on you. I think you must have been dreaming."

Dreaming?

I never actually *saw* the flask go black, did I? I never saw it pulse. When I did look at it, when light finally spilt into the room, it was just glassy, colourless, ordinary.

Though it had been blue. Fizz-heart, sky-happy blue.

I definitely saw that.

And I saw

the cork on the floor

and

the light that didn't travel in straight lines

and

the opalescence

and

the breathing and the flying

and

the little seed fish swimming

and…

"And that's before we get to your overactive imagination," Gran says. "Don't forget – you are the girl who invented Spike."

21

We don't go to the hospital. Mum says the twins have to have tests.

"Plenty of clearing to do at my house," says Gran.

She means Aunt Edie's house.

"That'll take our minds off things."

Her mind, maybe.

In the car over, I don't answer my phone when it rings. Gran doesn't like me answering the phone when we're in the middle of a conversation (although as it happens we're not in the middle of a conversation) because she says it's rude. But that's not the reason why I don't take my calls. I don't take them because they are all from Zoe. By the time we arrive I have four missed calls and a text: *soz. SOZ cll me. xx.*

Besides, I need to think about Spike. Spike is small

and blond and he never brushes his hair, so it's always wild and knotted. He comes with me everywhere, or at least he used to. He arrived when I grew out of ScatCat, sometimes smiling and full of jokes, sometimes irritating and demanding. He'd hide when I wanted to speak to him or shout out right at the moment I tried to ride my bike without stabilisers. He'd knock my juice over. But at night he was always calm, and came to bed with me, laid his head on the pillow beside mine. Only he never slept. He spent the whole night watching over me.

I'm here, Jess, right here.

Wacu. To be awake.

I'll never leave you.

To watch over.

I love you, Jess.

As Gran pulls up in her front drive, I realise I haven't been in her house since the day of the funeral. And I haven't been in the house next door – Aunt Edie's house – since Aunt Edie was there to open the door to me.

In Gran's porch is a blue-and-white china umbrella stand that used to be in Aunt Edie's porch. It makes my stomach lurch.

I love you, Jess.

"You'll never guess what I found," says Gran, leading

85

me straight past the umbrella stand that is in all the wrong place and into the dining room. "Look."

On the dining room table is a stack of Aunt Edie's photo albums, the sort that have real old-fashioned photos in, ones on glossy paper, not the flimsy pixilated ones you print off the computer.

She points at a picture of me aged about four pushing an empty swing. Beneath the photo, there is a scrap of paper on which is written, in Aunt Edie's loopy handwriting: *Jess and Spike.*

"Do you remember?"

Yes. For ever. I often pushed Spike on the swing. Spike liked the rhythm, it soothed him.

"For a whole three years, you wouldn't go anywhere without him," says Gran. "Jessica Walton and her imaginary friend, Spike." She laughs. "And the sandwiches you got Edie to make for him! Every time you had a plate, he had to have one too."

Then I remember something else. Aunt Edie made plates and plates of sandwiches for Spike – Marmite sandwiches, which were Spike's favourite. But Gran, she never gave Spike food. Not one sandwich in three years.

The place where I join with Aunt Edie burns.

22

Gran's and Aunt Edie's gardens are both shaped like witches' hats, wide close to the house and then narrowing to not much more than a compost heap where they back on to the park. The boundary between the two begins as a fence, making it quite clear which piece of land belongs to whom, but seventy feet further on there is just an increasingly tangled hedge where plants and boundary seem to twine together without end or beginning.

That makes me think of the twins and the web of their join and how they are both clearly separate and yet, beneath it all, they must tangle too.

The gate, which has a latch but no lock, is about a third of the way along, by Gran's eucalyptus tree. I know it is a eucalyptus because Aunt Edie would sometimes crush a leaf in her hand as we passed.

"Smell this, Jess."

The smell was pungent, fragrant, oily.

"That's my tree," Gran might say, in a tone that wasn't quite a joke. "And I'll thank you two to respect it."

"It's only a leaf," Aunt Edie would retort "Just one leaf."

They did bicker sometimes, Gran and Aunt Edie. Two increasingly old ladies: one who'd lost her husband early, one who'd never married. Sisters whose lives had joined along this boundary for over ten years.

Another pair of siblings joined.

I really hadn't thought about that before, but I think about it now, as Gran presses down on the latch and the gate swings open as it has so many times before.

Aunt Edie's house is to be sold. The gate will have to be locked, a bolt Gran's side, a bolt the side of the new neighbours. Gran will never go through that gate again. I will never go through it again. It makes me want to unlatch the gate and run back and forth a thousand times.

It also makes me want to ask Gran how she is, how she's feeling. Gran who has no husband and no son and now no sister. All her joins, her connections, broken. But I don't know how to open that conversation.

Gran shuts the gate behind her and puts a bony arm around my shoulder. And then, as if she can read my mind she says, "I feel so lucky to have you, Jess."

23

Gran opens the door of the glass lean-to (which Aunt Edie called the Sun Room) and we go in. The house smells damp and forgotten, as if it has been unlived in for years, not just for a couple of months.

I go straight into the drawing room which is where the piano is. The room runs the length of the house, and the piano is in the bay window to the front and the sofas around the fire to the rear. Only there aren't any sofas any more. All the large items of furniture have gone, leaving a rolled-up carpet, a few piles of books and Aunt Edie's ancient...

Ancient... there's Zoe again, nagging in my ear.

... ancient television. The piano, alone at the far end of the room, looks abandoned, cheerless. Its lid is down. Down! Aunt Edie's piano lid was never down.

"Who's going to have it?" I blurt out. "Who's getting Aunt Edie's piano? Where's it going?"

"It's not going anywhere," says Gran quickly. "Well, only next door."

"You're going to have it?" I must sound astonished.

"It's not that surprising," says Gran.

"But you don't play!"

"Ah, but you do. So instead of going to Aunt Edie's to play, you can come to mine, can't you?"

And I should be glad, I should be grateful. The piano isn't to be sold, isn't to go into some stranger's house. It will be just next door, I can play it any time I want. Any time I visit. But I just feel like someone threw a blanket over my head, hot and suffocated.

"Of course I'll have to make some space in my drawing room," says Gran. "Move things about, send a few more bits and bobs to auction. But it'll be worth it, Jess, to have you coming to play."

I can't meet her eyes, so I turn my back, go over to the piano, lift the lid and try a chord. Still in perfect tune.

"Are you pleased?" Gran asks.

"I love this piano," I say. This at least is true.

"Oh, and one more thing. Look." Gran scrabbles

beside the pile of books. "I found this."

It's a pile of music – Bach, Beethoven, Chopin, Mozart.

"Bit beyond you for the moment, probably," Gran says. "But practice makes perfect. You'll be needing to come round to my house a lot."

24

Gran hands me the music and goes off to *sort the vases*. I hear her clattering about in the kitchen.

Music.

Aunt Edie and I never used music. Notes have always filled me with fear. There, I've said it. Right from the beginning, they swam in front of my eyes. I never knew what lines they sat on, or why. I didn't understand the spaces or clefs or the time signatures.

"She doesn't seem to be making much progress," my mother reported.

Nor was I making much progress with reading. I was – I am – dyslexic, but nobody knew it then. Except perhaps Aunt Edie. Despite the fact she'd never even heard the word dyslexic, she just *knew*.

"Her music's all here," said Aunt Edie, tapping her

ears. "Where it should be. And also here." She tapped her heart.

It was Aunt Edie who suggested I give up learning with a conventional teacher and start learning the Suzuki way. She even managed to convince Si on the subject. The founder of the Suzuki method, Aunt Edie told him, observed how effortlessly Japanese children learnt their mother tongue. No one taught them their letters, they just listened to words and repeated them, like every other child in the world. A child could learn music the same way, said Shin'ichi Suzuki, by using his or her ears, by listening and then repeating. "*If a child hears fine music from the day of his birth and learns to play it himself,*" *said the master, "he develops sensitivity, discipline and endurance. He gets a beautiful heart.*"

So finding a slew of music books belonging to Aunt Edie feels like a betrayal. Which is stupid, because of course I know Aunt Edie could read music, even I can read some now, but I just don't want these books right now. I throw them on the floor. Concertos and sonatas and sonatinas skid about on the carpetless boards.

Then I sit down to play.

I play something very simple, a song we used to call 'Spring Garden'. "This is the grass growing," Aunt Edie would say. "And this, this is a cherry tree bursting into bloom. And these are the birds. Can you hear the birds, Jess?"

I didn't cry when they told me Aunt Edie was dead. I didn't cry at the funeral or at the wake. But when I hear those birds singing again, I sob my heart out.

25

After a while I stop playing and blow my nose. Then I think I should pick up the music books because Gran has never been very good at mess. There is the Beethoven, the Bach, the Mozart, the Chopin and a single sheet of paper. At first I think it's blank, because it's upside down, face to the floor. I am just about to slip it back inside *Chopin's Preludes* when I see that it is music too. A handwritten song, or a composition anyway, tiny little blue ink notes jumping about on neatly ruled (if fading) blue ink staves. The piece doesn't have a title, but in the top left-hand corner there is a dedication. In Aunt Edie's distinctive, loopy handwriting it says: *For Rob.*

This is even more of a shock to me than the books of music. Aunt Edie – writing a song down, committing it to paper? Aunt Edie who could remember every note of a piece, but who also liked to change things, experiment, improvise according to her mood – or mine.

And worse than this: Rob.

Who is Rob that Aunt Edie should dedicate a song to him? Something flashes hot across my heart.

Jealousy.

Aunt Edie and I made many songs together, but she never dedicated one for me. Never wrote it, fixed it down, put my name in blue at the top. *For Jess*.

I put the music on the piano stand, sit myself down, stare at the notes. I need to hear this piece, need to know what Aunt Edie has written to this Rob I've never heard of. I'm a good player, I really am, but I have to count the lines and spaces, try to find where the first ink dot lands. It makes me cross looking at all Aunt Edie's notes arranged in front of me like some locked-up treasure chest to which I do not have the key.

What grade are you on? That's what they always ask at school. And: *Did you get a merit or a distinction or just a pass?* Zoe's always doing dance exams, always getting distinctions. And even Em and Alice, who both do singing, get the odd merit or two. With Suzuki you don't do exams. And anyway – who cares? Who cares!

I've never wanted a piece of paper with some official stamp to say how good or bad I am. I've just wanted to be able to listen and then play the way Aunt Edie played. But today is different. Today I want to be able to sight-read, to recognise every note on the stave, be able to lift my hands to the keys and make immediate sense of the fading dots. What if they fade right away before my eyes, what if I never find out what Aunt Edie wrote to Rob? For Rob.

I try again. I find the first note, I check to see if there are any sharps or flats. I look for the rhythm. Minims or quavers? Notes with dots or notes without? Gradually I assemble a chord, and then another, and something in the base line too, a sad rocking sound. Then I think I hear something, catch something, like a melody coming by on the air, a haunting, hunted sound. And it's suddenly as if I can hear much more than I can play, a whole tune singing itself out loud. I stop playing and start listening and there it is, just as Aunt Edie always said it would be, a song in my ears, in my heart.

And also in my pocket.

The flask is singing. A song even sadder and stranger than the wolf lament of the previous night – and bigger too. Much bigger – a huge song. Something that makes me feel that this is how God would have sung if, when he called the world into being, when he made the stars and the seas and the land and the lions, when he crafted each spark of sky, each drop of water, each blade of grass and every single hair in the lion's mane, he also knew that, one day, the stars would burn out, the seas dry up and the land and the lions die.

I draw out the flask, oh so slowly, because it feels unholy to disturb this song.

You know how it is sometimes when you see someone crying and you know you can't comfort them? That even if you put your arm around them, it won't make any difference, they just have to cry till they're finished with it? That's how the song is making me feel.

I stand the flask on the piano. Its heart is swirling, grey and purple, the colour of storm clouds and bruises. Gently, I unwind the sticky tape from the throat of glass, not to hear the song better – I could hear it if I was the other side of the world – but just because I think the song, the flask, needs to be free.

Then of course my hands begin to find the notes. I can just lay my hands on the piano and feel the music flow out of my fingers. I can play the sadness, play the stars and the seas and the land and the lions.

"How do you know that tune?" Gran is suddenly in the doorway, statue still, face like she's seen a ghost.

My hands falter, they fall from the notes. The spell breaks.

"Where did you get that music?"

"Found it," I say. "With the other music. Aunt Edie's music."

"I haven't heard that since…" Her voice dies away.

"Since what?" I ask. "Since when?"

She unlocks, comes across the room, her footsteps hollow on the bare floorboards. "Never you mind," she says.

"But it's such beautiful music."

"Beautiful!" she exclaims. She stops in front of the stand and stares at the faded notes.

"And sad," I say, "really sad. Who's Rob, Gran?"

Gran says nothing.

"It says *For Rob*," I repeat.

"Does it." And Gran takes the sheet of music and she folds it, no, she crushes up that paper and puts it in her pocket. "And what," she adds suddenly and just to change the subject, "is that?"

26

It's the flask.

But it isn't swirling with storm clouds and bruises; it's just its quiet, colourless self.

"It's a bottle," I say.

"Where did you get it from?" Gran asks.

"Just found it."

"You seem to be finding a lot of things, Jess."

"It was in the desk. Aunt Edie's desk."

"I thought I cleared that bureau," says Gran, and then I see her hand lift and the bottle becomes my precious flask and I know I don't want her to touch it. I like my gran, I really do, but I just don't want her to touch Aunt Edie's flask.

My flask.

"No," I cry.

But just before Gran's fingers reach the glass, there's that whoosh again, that wind got up from nowhere, and into the air comes whatever it is that lies in the flask. The living, breathing thing, whirling and trembling. I hear it, so Gran must hear it too. Only she doesn't, so her fingers kept reaching, they close around the neck of the bottle.

And the whooshing breath, that big-as-a-storm-wind, tiny-as-a-baby's-snuffle breath, it comes eddying and circling towards me, and I stretch out my hands and suddenly it's between my palms. I can feel it beating there, like a trapped butterfly.

And for two seconds, or maybe two hundred years, I hold myself like a sheet of glass, terrified that, with a single movement, I could crush that breath for ever, though some other part of me feels that, for all its trembling, that beating is the strongest thing in the world.

27

Finally, Gran puts down the bottle. "The things my sister kept," she says.

At once the butterfly breath flies and curls itself straight back inside the flask.

I look at Gran's face. She has seen nothing, heard nothing. How is it possible for people to see and hear nothing?

"Well, enough time-wasting," Gran says and smiles, as though we were both having the most ordinary of days. "Come on, we've got jobs to do."

I slip the flask back inside my pocket and Gran sets me to work. I dry the vases she's washed; sort the good tools from the broken ones in Aunt Edie's shed; help her lift things like the old coal scuttle that are too heavy for her alone. And actually it feels good to be doing some helpful, simple things. Although maybe the joy is to do with the flask because I'm no longer afraid that, without a cork, without sticky tape, the butterfly breath will fly away.

Because it chose me, didn't it?

It sheltered under my hand.

28

It's about four o'clock before we set off home.

I have another text from Zoe. She reminds me that tomorrow is the day we're going – with Paddy – to the Buddhist Centre for our holiday project on Places of Worship. Will I just text her back to say I haven't forgotten?

We are going with Paddy because Zoe was in charge of the arrangements and she deliberately arranged the visit on a day she knew that Em and Alice were both going to be away and Paddy wasn't. Zoe told me this was just an oversight, but I didn't believe it then and I don't believe it now.

I don't text her back. This is what my mother, who is a very gentle person, calls *bearing a grudge*.

"Si phoned," says Gran in the car. "He's coming back

tonight. Check I'm feeding you properly."

As Gran plans to sleep in her own house that night, I wonder why it is that she's driving me home, why Si hasn't come to collect me. I think Gran wonders this too when we pull into our drive to find the garage doors open and Si on his back underneath the Morris Traveller 1000.

"Oh, for goodness' sake," Gran says as she pulls up.

Hearing us arrive, Si slides out from underneath the car. He is lying on a little trolley, a wooden platform on casters which he made himself.

He looks like a daddy-long-legs, too thin and sprawly for the platform. He's tall, Si, and bony, and has springy, sandy-coloured hair. I'm not particularly tall for my age, but I'm also a bit bony and have that same sandy-coloured hair. We also both have greyish eyes.

Don't you and your dad look alike! Lots of people have said that to me. I don't tell them Si's my stepfather, it just causes complications. In fact there have been many times when I've pretended that Si is my father. It makes things easier, like at school, when they ask you to write stuff about your family. What does your father do for a living? My father's a mechanic. Actually Si is not a mechanic, but he might as well be, the amount of time he spends on this car.

He has been working on his 'little moggie' pretty much the whole time he's been in my life. Him and the oily cardboard and the spare parts and the spanners and the tinkering. *Tinkering.* That's what Mum calls it, though she says it lovingly.

"You'd think he could leave it alone for one day," says Gran. "With everything that's going on."

"Hello Angela," says Si, as she gets out of the car. Then he swivels round to face me. "Hi Jess. How's tricks?"

The trolley on which he swivels is my fault. If I had been the stepchild he wanted, it would have been Si lying – trolleyless – under the car tinkering and me lying beside him. Me being interested in exhausts, radiators, crankshafts, timing chains and me wriggling out to fetch whatever bolt or socket spanner he had forgotten, so he could keep lying there, hour after hour. And it's not that I haven't tried to be interested, I have. I just never quite got the point of Roger the Wreck. Yes, that's what he calls it – Roger the Wreck. Because when he bought it, it wasn't really a car at all, more a sort of heap of junk. But over the years he's lovingly put it all back together again. He's screwed and bolted and joined and greased it into some sort of whole, bursting with the pride of it.

"Fit like a glove, don't they, Jess? The new doors."

But actually there's still a gale-force draught around those doors and the word new would not pass a lie detector. There is nothing new about this car. All its components, the wood frame, the chrome trims, the headlamps, they all come from the other cars, the 'donor' cars, which squat in our garage. Other heaps of junk which he raids to make Roger run. Roger who occasionally roars into life sounding, Mum says, like a war-time Spitfire.

I was nine when Si made himself the little trolley on caster wheels, nine when he finally admitted to himself that, as a mechanic's assistant, I was a failure. That, if he forgot the socket spanner (the heavy one from the Britool box marked *war issue*) he would have to crawl out from under the car and get it himself. The trolley made things easier – he could just scoot in and out – but, whenever I see it, I can't help feeling his sense of disappointment.

"How are the babies?" asks Gran pointedly, as though a real man would not be tinkering under a car when his newborn babies are lying tangled up in a hospital cot.

"Heart ultrasound, EKG. CT scans. Blood work. Even skin tests – mouths and noses checked for bacteria and fungi and…" He suddenly pauses. "They're fighting," he says. "They're giving it everything they've got."

And his eyes go fierce and starry again, not like the Si I know, and do you know what? That red hotness flashes across my chest a second time in one day. And I imagine how it would be if the twins come home and lie under the Morris Traveller 1000 and pass their father (their *father*) the war-issue socket spanner. And because there are two of them, one could always be under the car and the other hopping about for the spanner, so they'd never have to leave him and he wouldn't be disappointed ever again. And, of course, I know I'm being ridiculous. I'm being totally unfair on these two babies, who might not even make it to being grown-up enough to get under a car, and in any case, just because they're boys it doesn't mean they'll be any more interested than me in oil and grease and dungarees but, but… would he have really wanted them if I'd been good enough? If there'd never been a trolley?

And then it hits me. I've separated them, haven't I? I've put a knife down their join and I've put one twin under the car and the other hopping about for spanners. And of course there's been talk in our house about separation. But it's so risky, so delicate, that even Si hasn't talked so very loudly about it. And here I am, just dividing them willy-nilly, sticking the knife in. Statistic: since 1950, seventy per cent of separations result in one live twin.

One.

Just one.

"I don't suppose you've thought about dinner?" Gran says.

"Takeaway?" hazards Si.

Gran rolls her eyes, as though this is the most ludicrous thing she's ever heard, and then marches into the house to rustle something up.

Which leaves me just standing there.

Si looks up. "All right, Jess?" he says and then, with an expert kick of his left heel, he disappears under the car.

29

Si would have preferred takeaway, I would have preferred takeaway, but we get rice and frozen vegetables and leftover (Zoe would say *pre-owned*) chicken. Instead of discussing the babies, we talk, or rather Gran talks, about adventures with vases and coal scuttles and garden sheds. I say nothing and Si doesn't say much either.

"Hope it hasn't been too dull for you," Si says, as Gran's car finally pulls out of the drive.

"Gran told me about Clem's little dip," I jump in straightaway with this, because part of me fears that Si will disappear under the car again. Or back to the hospital. Or just disappear plain and simple.

"Hmm?" says Si.

"Dip – in the night."

"Oh. The murmur. Clem has a VSD, a ventricle septal

defect — what they used to call a 'hole in the heart'. So there was a bit of a dip in his breathing last night. Monitor went off. But lots of kids have holes like these apparently — and they can often spontaneously resolve. So we're not worrying too much about that at the moment."

"What time did the monitor go off?"

"I don't know, somewhere round two o'clock, I think. Why?"

You look frozen, Jess. Come on now, back to bed, it's gone two o'clock.

"Are there explanations for everything, Si?" I ask then.

"You mean real ones, scientific ones?"

When I was about five, someone apparently asked me, in Mum's hearing, what 'Si' was short for. And I didn't reply *Simon*, I replied *science*. That became a family joke for a while, though I never found it very funny.

"Yes," I say, even though it's not really what I mean at all.

"There are explanations for everything we've been clever enough to work out so far," Si says. "But there's still a whole lot of stuff we don't really understand still. Which is why people still believe in God."

God again.

"Or gods," he goes on.

I prepare myself for his Best Explaining Voice, though I only have myself to blame.

"Take Helios," Si says. "The Greek sun god who was supposed to drag his four-horsed chariot across the sky each morning and with it the rising sun. Each night, the ancients believed he, rather conveniently, travelled back to the east in a golden cup ready to ride across the sky the following day. That story lasted pretty much until we discovered that actually it's the earth's rotation that causes night and day. After which, Helios was out of a job."

This is quite interesting, and it's also not nearly as involved as Si's usual explanations, so I think he must be tired. In fact, when I actually look at him, he seems exhausted. So I hurry up, and I tell him about waking up at the exact moment that Clem's heart was murmuring.

"Gran said it was just worry…" I start.

"Reasonable enough," says Si. "Though you'd also have to consider simple coincidence."

I consider it. If the flask is in some way connected to the twins, then how can it also be connected to this Rob person, or at least to the song Aunt Edie wrote for him? So maybe the howling and the waking up was just coincidence. But then again, coincidences don't normally crush your heart up.

"Coincidence is a perfectly rational explanation," says Si. "Not everything happens for a reason, you know."

My face must not be liking this answer because he goes on. "Trouble is, human beings seem to be wired to believe just the opposite. We find it difficult to accept that things can be random. That stuff just happens."

Stuff, I suppose, like Aunt Edie writing a really important song to someone I've never heard of. Just some random piece of nothing. And I'm just about to ask Si who this nothing, random Rob is, when I realise there is no way Si will know because Si and Edie – they're not even part of the same family.

So instead I say, "I don't think everything does come down to science."

"What?" says Si.

"I mean," I say, keeping calm enough to choose my example with care, "I mean, when you're in a car, just driving along and suddenly you just feel there's someone looking at you and you turn around, and there in the next car, there is, there's someone staring at you. That's not science, is it?"

"Sixth sense," says Si. "That's what that is." He smiles. "Which is just another way of saying, we can't explain it *yet*. Bit like Helios. Maybe in a hundred or two hundred years' time – then we'll have an explanation for car staring as well."

It's his smile, his smug smile, that makes me take the flask out and put it on the kitchen table.

"What would you say," I ask and it all comes out in a rush, "if I told you that, when Clem's heart was murmuring, this old bottle started pulsing, started howling, like some wolf, crying and howling and pushing black black stuff into my bedroom and it wasn't a dream, it really wasn't. And what if I told you that the flask can sing as well, that it can sing something bigger than God, bigger than planets and—"

"Jess, Jess, steady." He puts his big bony arm around my shoulder. Then he says he's sorry.

"Sorry?"

"We've all been taken up, haven't we, with the twins."

"It's not that!"

And I'm probably furious because I shouldn't be

talking to him about this sort of stuff. I should be talking to Zoe, my beautiful dancing, mirror-image friend Zoe. Only I've pushed her away, haven't I? I'm all busy hating her and pushing her away when I've never needed her more than I do now. So it's all my fault that I'm alone with Si and a flask that doesn't make any sense.

Si picks up the bottle.

I wait for the whoosh, the breath and the butterfly beating under my hands. But nothing happens. The bottle, the flask, is still.

He turns it around in his hands.

"It's a beautiful thing," he says. "Eighteenth century. Whisky flask, if I'm not mistaken. They're called pumpkin seed flasks, I think, because of their shape."

He is giving it a name, he's describing it, making it just some stupid historical object.

"You don't understand!" I shout.

"I'm a parent," says Si. "That's my job."

"You're not my parent," I shout.

I have never said this to Si before.

Ever.

Si moves a little closer. "Jess," he says. "Jess, it's all right."

But it isn't.

30

The following morning, Paddy's mother arrives in our drive at 10.30 a.m. Paddy's sitting in the front seat of the car and Zoe's in the back.

"Our big day at the Buddhist Centre with Onion Bhaji," announces Paddy.

"Not onion bhaji," said Mrs Paddy. "Lalitavajri." Mrs Paddy has a name of her own – Sarah, I think – but everyone calls her Mrs Paddy because she just looks like a bigger, smilier version of Paddy himself. That big, round cheerful beach ball face.

I look at Paddy. He's grinning. I don't think he remembers anything that happened in the park. I don't think he remembers that I would have liked to beat him to death. Zoe does remember. There's something flickering and anxious about her.

"In you get," says Mrs Paddy.

I get in. I'm carrying my clipboard and my Places of Worship questionnaire.

"Hi Jess," says Zoe.

I look out of the window.

"As it's Easter," Mum said before she went into hospital, "I don't know why you can't visit a Christian place of worship."

"It's to broaden our minds," I told her.

"Going in a Christian church would probably broaden most of your lot's minds," Si remarked.

The truth, which I didn't tell them, is that we could have chosen a church or a temple or a mosque, for that matter. We probably would have chosen a church if Em or Alice had been part of our group. But, thanks to Zoe and the issue of the holiday dates, they got paired with Jack and we got Paddy.

"I vote for Buddhism," Paddy said. "Father Neville knows a big fat zero about Buddhism, so I reckon we'll be on safe ground whatever we write."

"How're things with the babies, Jess?" Mrs Paddy asks, as we head out of the close.

"Fine," I say.

"And your mum?"

"Fine."

"Well, give her my very best, won't you?"

I say I will and then Mrs Paddy leaves the subject. Sometimes you have to be grateful for adults.

Zoe then asks Paddy if he's seen some new film and it turns out he has, and she stops being anxious and flickering and starts one of those conversations that go: "Oh, my gosh, wasn't it amazing when…", "Yeah, but did you see – wow, I mean…" And they're completely involved in the excitement of it all and I'm still staring out of the window. Which is, of course, entirely my own fault.

"You haven't seen the film yet then, Jess?" says Mrs Paddy, picking up on my silence.

And I know the yet is just to let me off the hook, to make it clear that I'm not really some excluded saddo, it's just that I haven't seen the film yet.

"No," I say. "Not yet."

"Bit too much going on at your house probably," says Mrs Paddy kindly.

Bit too much going on in my mind.

About a million years later we arrive at the Buddhist Centre.

"Do you know what this building used to be?" Mrs

Paddy asks, as we draw up.

"No," I say. Paddy and Zoe are still on the film.

"An old shoe factory," says Mrs Paddy.

We tip out on to the street.

"I'll be back for you in an hour," says Mrs Paddy.

The double doors to the centre open on to a small porch with hooks for coats and racks for shoes. Beyond this the ground floor is divided into an open-plan office, a library, a tiny kitchen and a reception area with comfy chairs and cushions and rugs which looks like someone's sitting room. We all hesitate long enough in the porch for someone to ask us our business and suggest we remove our shoes.

"We've come to see," Paddy pauses, "Lalitavajri."

"Ah, that's me." A small, smiling woman with oceans of curly orange hair rises from one of the comfy chairs. "You must be Maxim."

Paddy nods. "And this is Zoe, and Jess."

"Welcome," says Lalitavajri. "You're all very welcome." Her orange curls bob as she talks. "Shall we go to the Shrine Room then?"

We follow her up three flights of stairs, passing a number of small rooms and shut doors, so the Shrine Room is a surprise. It runs the full length of the building, a spacious airy room with a huge skylight beyond which frothy white clouds scud across the sky. At the far end of the room, where the altar would be in a church, there's a golden screen painted with the image of the Buddha, and arranged simply on the floor in front of him, are some candles and vases of flowers. The flowers don't look shop bought, they look like they've been cut from people's gardens. There are a couple of branches, heavy with pink cherry blossom, some hyacinths in a jam jar and a vase with some tall bell-shaped flowers I don't know the name of. There are also three bendy stems of eucalyptus.

Yes, eucalyptus.

Si would probably say it's just a coincidence that some of the fragrant, oily leaves that Aunt Edie pressed for me to smell, are here in this room where I've only come because Zoe wanted to do the project with Paddy and Paddy thinks our RE teacher is a goon, but it doesn't feel that way to me. It feels that this room is welcoming me. And then I think a bit more about coincidences. Was it a coincidence that instead of getting Aunt Edie's piano I got the bureau and inside the bureau was the flask? And was it a coincidence that I found that flask? Or was that to do with my real father, whose slide rule wouldn't fit? And was it a coincidence that Gran gave me that slide rule in the first place? How far can you trace back these so-called coincidences? All the things that might have happened but didn't because you made this choice, not that one. All the coincidences that have led me into this room with the eucalyptus. And then I wish I'd brought the flask with me, instead of leaving it behind in my bedroom, thinking that this project was just some homework thing and not part of my real life. Maybe the flask would have had something to say about the eucalyptus.

"Now," says Lalitavajri, "how do you want to do this?"

"We've got a questionnaire," says Paddy, waving it as though it's a map of the known universe.

Lalitavajri sits down on a mat beside a golden gong and invites us to sit beside her.

"Fire away," she says.

"What drew you personally to Buddhism?" reads Paddy solemnly.

"Ah, that's easy," says Lalitavajri. "A world where kindness and generosity have the highest value."

And straightaway I feel bad, because here I am sitting cross-legged in this beautiful Shrine Room and a large part of me is still bearing a grudge against Zoe. And Paddy for that matter. And Si who calls himself my father, but is actually only the babies' father. And the babies themselves for being so dangerously muddled up together. And, actually, against myself. I'm bearing a grudge against myself for being so stupid and never letting go, and...

"And what for you is the most important belief in Buddhism?" asks Zoe.

"That we can change," says Lalitavajri. "That each one of us can be the most compassionate person we can be."

This hits me like a thrown stone. Or maybe it's not Lalitavajri's words, maybe it's Zoe's glance that hits me. I'm not looking at Zoe, but she's looking at me. She's giving me one of those totally non-scientific stares, which bangs right into the heart of things.

The heart of me.

"Now," says Lalitavajri, "do you want to know about the statues?"

According to Paddy's list, we do. Also on his list are pujas, gongs and drums.

"And what's that?" asks Paddy.

"Incense," says Lalitavajri. "We use incense because

it smells beautiful and, most importantly, it blows in all directions, like a smile. If you smile at someone they feel happy and then they smile at someone else. Incense passes on like this."

Paddy smirks, but Lalitavajri smiles and Zoe smiles back. Quite a shy smile for someone so big and so bold and actually – now I look at her – so beautiful. I don't know if I'm smiling, but I really hope I am.

"How do you think your shrine reflects the Buddhist faith?" reads Paddy.

"Can I ask you first how the Shrine Room strikes you?" Lalitavajri asks.

"Well, it's kind of big," says Paddy. "And empty, you know, compared with a church."

"And peaceful," I say. I'm still looking at Zoe. "Somewhere you can think."

And now Zoe feels my look and she lifts her eyes to me, all hesitant and hopeful at the same time.

"I like that," says Lalitavajri. "Western life is so busy we need a space to be peaceful. Buddhists choose for their shrines whatever's beautiful and makes them happy."

My gaze moves, it finds the eucalyptus branches and therefore, Aunt Edie.

"Is that what the flowers are for?" I ask. "Beauty?"

"Yes," says Lalitavajri. "And they also symbolise impermanence. Nothing lives for ever. All things die."

Aunt Edie again.

And also Zoe. My friendship with her. Am I going to let that die?

No.

Never.

"What do Buddhists believe happens after you die?" I ask.

Paddy looks confused. This question is not on our sheet.

"We believe in rebirth," says Lalitavajri. "After you die you go into a state of life between life, which we call *bardo*, like night is the bardo between two days, or a dream is a bardo between two wakings."

"A join?" I say. "Do you mean a join?"

"I'm not sure about that," says Lalitavajri. "But your body falls away and your consciousness remains."

"And what happens to that consciousness?"

"It remains until it is attracted to a man and a woman having sex," says Lalitavajri, "then it goes into the soul and enters the baby."

At the word *sex* Paddy sniggers.

But Lalitavajri just goes on: "This is why babies arrive with personalities already formed."

And I'm still thinking about the bardo which (whatever Lalitavajri says) does sound like a Buddhist version of a join, and about the knotted threads of friendship and about how a consciousness might remain when Paddy says, "Do you mean souls hang about, you know, like ghosts, they haunt you?"

"Not haunt, no. Although Buddhism does stretch the Western idea of the rational. Like some Buddhists have claimed to be able to walk through walls."

"Walk through walls!"

"I don't disbelieve this," says Lalitavajri. "Just as you can have déjà vu about someone coming into a room and then they come into a room."

Or you can have someone look at you and feel that look.

"Ghosts and the supernatural," Lalitavajri continues, "are much more real for people in the East."

And for me. And for the flask.

Paddy is scribbling in his notebook.

"Well, is that it?" asks Lalitavajri.

"Yes," says Zoe. "Thanks. Except – what does your name mean, Lalitavajri?"

"When you're ordained you are given a new name by the person who ordains you," says Lalitavajri. "You don't know your name until this moment. You are named either for things you have achieved or for the potential seen in you. *Lalita* means *she who plays* and *vajri* means *diamond thunderbolt*. The diamond thunderbolt represents reality, the truth and unstoppable energy."

"Wow," says Paddy, looking up from his notes. "So if I was a Buddhist I could get called Supreme Striker, or something?"

"Well, maybe not something so…" Lalitavajri pauses, "… specific."

"You could be called Paddy though," says Zoe and laughs. But she's not laughing at him, she's just laughing because everything suddenly feels relaxed, easy.

"Sorry?" says Lalitavajri.

"They call me Paddy," says Paddy. "Because…" He looks at Zoe. "Why do people call me Paddy?"

And Zoe laughs some more and Paddy grins in his Happy-to-Be-the-Centre-of-Attention way, and I feel a strange warmth wash through me, which takes in, without judgment, Zoe and Paddy and Aunt Edie and the supernatural and ghosts and souls.

"Well, I need to prepare now," says Lalitavajri. "I

have to lead a meditation in a minute. Although, you'd be welcome to stay if you'd like. A meditation would give you a very good idea of Buddhist practice."

Paddy's face suggests that the last thing in the world he'd like to do is stay for a Buddhist meditation.

"No," he says. "Thanks. I think my mum will be back for us any minute now."

"Well, another time," says Lalitavajri. "I'm here every Tuesday if you want to change your mind."

And I think, yes... I'm going to come back here.

And I'm going to bring the flask.

31

"Well?" asks Mrs Paddy. "How was it?"

"Buddhism," says Paddy, "is mental."

"Mental?" repeats Mrs Paddy.

Paddy consults his notes. "Buddhists," he reads, "claim to be able to walk through walls. 'I don't disbelieve this.' That's what she said, Onion Bhaji: 'I don't disbelieve this.'"

Mrs Paddy laughs. "Bit like Christians then."

"What?" says Paddy.

"Well," says Mrs Paddy, "Christians believe that, three days after being crucified, a man rose to life again."

"That's different," says Paddy.

"Is it?" says Mrs Paddy.

"Course," replies Paddy. "Christianity's true."

"Oh," says Mrs Paddy. "Says who?"

"Father Neville!" says Paddy, like he's just played the Ace of Spades.

Mrs Paddy keeps quiet.

"Anyway, it not just the walls stuff," continues Paddy. "There's plenty of other weird stuff in Buddhism."

"Such as?"

"Such as after you die, your soul hangs about until, until…"

"Until?"

"Until a man and a woman have sex," adds Zoe helpfully.

Paddy sniggers and Zoe beams, as if the joke is all hers.

"And then," Paddy adds, "your soul goes into the baby which means…"

"Everyone gets a pre-owned soul," concludes Zoe.

Then they both laugh and things seem to be going back to the way they were with the conversation about films.

"Isn't that horrible?" says Paddy. "I mean, having someone else's soul inside you? How creepy is that?"

"But if it was in you," I say, maybe just because I'm beginning to wish I was back in the Shrine Room where all things seemed possible, "it wouldn't be someone else's, it'd be yours."

"It would still be pre-owned," says Zoe.

Pre-owned is clearly going to take over from ancient as Zoe's new favourite word.

"Pre-owned," considers Mrs Paddy.

"You know, like in an X-box game or a DVD that used to belong to someone else."

"Oh," says Mrs Paddy, "you mean second-hand."

"Pre-owned," repeats Zoe. "Disgusting. Yuck, yuck, yuck."

"Hang on," says Mrs Paddy. "We're all a bit second-h— pre-owned, if you think about it."

"What?" says Paddy.

"What?" says Zoe.

"Well, genetics," says Mrs Paddy. "Like you have your dad's eye colour, Maxim, and my face shape and your grandad's laugh, and you don't think of that as disgusting, do you?"

Paddy looks like, all of a sudden, he's not quite so sure about this.

"So why would it seem so strange," Mrs Paddy adds, "to share a soul with someone?"

I look at Mrs Paddy trying to work out whether she believes what she's saying or is just doing what Si calls Playing Devil's Advocate, which is saying stuff you don't believe just for the sake of A Discussion. I decide she's being truthful.

"Well, it might not even be the soul of someone in your family," says Paddy. "I mean, you might get the soul of an ant."

Paddy having the soul of an ant could explain a lot of things.

"I didn't know Buddhism did the animal thing," says Mrs Paddy. "Are you sure about that?"

"Or what if it was the ants who were having sex?" says Zoe (and I'm hoping sex isn't going to become her new word). "I mean, that would be even worse. You'd end up inside the ant."

"On the other hand," says Paddy, "you'd probably be so much cleverer than all the other ants, you'd be Ant Emperor and then you could marshal the forces of ants worldwide and take over the universe."

"Who says souls are clever?" says Mrs Paddy.

"What?" says Paddy.

"What?" says Zoe.

"Well, souls can be many things," says Mrs Paddy, "but I'm not sure clever is one of them."

I'm beginning to change my mind about Mrs Paddy.

Other than Si (who's a life form that would probably baffle even Pug), most adults I know talk about Nothing in Particular. They can talk about Nothing in Particular for hours on end: homework, washing-up, road tax, the education system, lawnmowers, lost keys, the supermarket run and here is Mrs Paddy, who I've always thought of as simply a larger version of Paddy, actually being interesting. Thoughtful, even. I'm not sure I should be calling her Mrs Paddy any more. I think I should be calling her Sarah, because even if it turns out that she has a pre-owned soul, I think she definitely has a brain all of her own.

"What do you mean?" I ask her.

"Well, you hear of 'old souls', don't you?" says Sarah. "Sometimes people look into the eyes of babies and say, 'Well, here's an old soul', as though that baby has some sort of wisdom they couldn't possibly have unless they'd been round once or twice before. But 'clever' souls – I don't know."

"What's the difference between being clever and being wise?" asks Paddy.

"Quite a lot," says Sarah.

32

When we get back to the house, it's Gran who opens the door. Si has obviously returned to the hospital. Gran invites Sarah in for tea and that leaves me with Zoe – but also with Paddy. I wish Paddy would just Go Away, I wish he'd disappear in a Puff of Smoke. It's so difficult to think around someone who treats the whole universe as a joke. And I need to do some thinking and I need to check in with Zoe, to see how we are.

I also need to be with the flask.

But Zoe's already bounding up the stairs to my bedroom and Paddy's following her, and I'm following both of them.

Why am I always following people?

It's Zoe, of course, who's first into the room.

"Wow," she says. "Will you look at that!"

We look.

As I managed to get up and leave the house this morning without opening the curtains, there is nothing in my room but darkness.

Nothing, that is, but the flask.

The flask is sitting on my computer table, swirling clouds and clouds of fluorescent green.

And Zoe is looking straight at it.

Zoe can see the flask – she can see inside it!

"Jeez," says Paddy. "That's amazing!"

And Paddy – Paddy can see inside it too.

Paddy!

I feel something thrill up my spine. I am not alone. I am not alone! They can see it. I am not going mad. I am not the only person in the universe who can see beyond science, beyond Si, just… beyond. And, all at once, I love Zoe! I even love Paddy.

"What on earth is it?" Paddy is advancing into the room, making for the green swirl of the flask.

Zoe moves too, she's almost dancing towards the glow. But I remain where I am, stuck in the doorway, because suddenly I think there's something wrong, something unholy about the flask and its colour. It's not making me feel good, not like the fizz-heart blue.

It's coming to me slowly, oh so slowly across the room. I'm fighting to think exactly what it is that's wrong and then I get it: up until now the flask has only held natural colours, the iridescence of pearls, the blue of the sky, the grey of storm clouds, the purple of bruises, the black of night. This green is alien, lurid, electric.

Paddy arrives at the computer table. He stretches out his hand.

"Wait," I cry.

But he's already lifting the flask, holding it in his hands.

"Oh, you're joking," he exclaims.

At desk level are the four flashing, fluorescent green lights of my broadband internet connection. In his hands is a colourless flask.

"It's just a stupid old bottle," he says.

"Give it here," says Zoe.

He gives it to her, all interest gone. She places it down in front of the broadband connection again, watches the clouds gather and swirl, the green computer lights refracted through the uneven contours of the glass. Then she picks the flask up, puts it down again, just to check.

"Oh," she says, equally disappointed. "Just for a

moment I thought we might all have walked through a wall, actually found something special, a genie in a bottle. Wouldn't that have been something?"

"Me," I say. I've begun to unlock, I'm going across that room faster than light. "Give it to me!"

"Steady on," says Paddy, sensing my urgency. "It's not going anywhere."

But it is going somewhere. In fact it's already gone. I know even before I lay my hands on the bottle, the flask is empty. The butterfly breath has gone.

33

I snatch the flask from Zoe's hands, stare down its glass throat, just like I did when I couldn't believe the cork was missing.

"There's nothing in there," says Paddy, as though I'm a total imbecile. "It was just the lights. The lights of the computer."

"But what if it had been for real?" says Zoe. "Imagine that. Our very own genie. We could have asked for whatever we wanted."

"Correction," says Paddy, "I could have asked for whatever I wanted. I was the one that touched it first, you know, as in me – master, you – slave."

"Not me slave," says Zoe. "Genie – slave."

"No," I roar. "Not a slave. Not now, not ever. The biggest, freest, most extraordinary being in the universe."

"What?" says Paddy.

"What?" says Zoe.

"In this bottle, in this flask. Big as a storm wind, tiny as a baby's breath. It was here!"

Zoe and Paddy exchange glances.

They think I've lost it.

Paddy puts his head to one side. "Jess," he says solemnly, "did you bang your head when you stepped through one of those Buddhist walls?"

And Zoe laughs.

She *laughs*.

"Tell you what," adds Paddy, "why don't we shed some light on this sad little scene?" He opens the curtains.

And there it is, there on the window sill, like some curled, pearly cat.

"Look," I shriek, spilt over with happiness. "Look!"

They look.

"Oh," says Paddy. "I see."

He sees!

He leans forward, putting his hand straight through the pearly cat, and knocks on the windowpane.

"Sam," he yells. "Look, it's Sam!"

Zoe joins him at the window. The pearly cat has

reformed, close to the glass, but away from Paddy's huge, clumsy hands. Zoe will see it, surely Zoe will see it?

She looks straight at the pulsing light, straight through it, out over the rooftops, down the street and towards the rising mound of the park.

"And Alice," she says. "That's Alice with him, isn't it?"

"Yeah," says Paddy. "Come on – what are we waiting for?"

Paddy isn't waiting for much, he's straight off down the stairs and Zoe would be with him, with hardly a backwards glance, only I grab her elbow.

"Wait!" I cry.

"Huh?"

"Don't go," I say.

"Why?"

I mean to say, *There's so much I need to share with you*. And, *Please, because it's scary having to deal with this all by myself*.

What I actually say is, "Don't go. Don't go with him."

"With Paddy?"

"Yes. No. I mean it, please." And I give her one of those looks that, between friends, don't usually need words. The one that says simply: *Be there for me*.

"You're not making sense," says Zoe.

"Wait," I say again, unwilling to let go of her arm in case she just runs straight out of my life, but needing to get something from the bureau. I scrabble behind the arched door flanked by the two wooden pillars. "Look."

She looks. I'm showing her the braided bracelet of pink and purple she made for me in year 5.

"So?" she says.

"Best friends," I say. "That's what you said. When I wanted to wind Em in, when I wanted to make a bracelet for all three of us. 'Don't you understand about best friends?' That's what you said."

"I was nine," says Zoe, incredulous. "Ten, tops. What are you talking about?"

"Zoe!" yells Paddy from the front door.

"Look, either come or don't," says Zoe. "I don't care one way or the other. But don't go all heavy on me. Since when were we joined at the hip?"

34

I stand stunned. Loneliness never felt this big or close before. If it wasn't for the relief of getting rid of Paddy, I'd cry.

"Are you OK?" I finally manage to ask the iridescent breath on the window sill.

No reply.

"I'm sorry about, you know, Paddy's hand."

No reply.

"He's got stupidly big hands. Should really be a goalie, not a striker." I'm making light of it, but it doesn't feel light.

"Why do you go there?" I ask then. "To the window sill?"

No reply.

"You're not a, you know, consciousness, are you?"

In the Shrine Room the concept of a consciousness sounded quite reasonable, ordinary even. In my bedroom it sounds ridiculous.

"Or a soul," I try. "An old soul. Like Mrs Paddy said?"

No reply.

Sometimes I think I made up not just Spike, but half of the universe. The half that doesn't fit.

You're not making sense. *You're not making sense.*

I go to the window myself. Look out. Paddy and Zoe are already halfway down the street.

On the window sill, the butterfly breath continues to pulse quietly.

"Are you looking for something? Well, I know you can't look exactly…" Do I know that? What I mean is, I can't explain how something without eyes can look, but then I can't explain déjà vu, or the car staring thing or…

The breath seems quite calm, but I feel that it must keep going to the window sill for a reason.

Not everything happens for a reason.

Shut up, Si.

Perhaps what I'm really saying is that if it were me with my nose pressed up against the glass, then I'd be looking out, wouldn't I? I'd be searching for something.

Trapped behind glass (the glass of the flask, the glass of the windowpane), I'd be all full of longing.

"What is it you want?" I ask. "What are you looking for?"

No reply.

"Or is it who? Who are you looking for? Is it Rob?"

No reply.

"Who is Rob, anyhow?"

No reply.

"If I knew what you wanted," I hear myself say, "I'd find it. I'd give it."

The light trembles. No, it shimmers, all of the colours inside it increasing in intensity.

Part of me wants to touch each of those shimmering pearly colours, the vivid threads of blues and greens, the opalescent pinks and whites. Touch them not with some fat fist, but just with the lightest of fingertips, to give some reassurance, to say: I am here. I am with you – as Spike was for me. Although this urge to touch also feels intrusive, like touching the join between my brothers. So I put my hands together, cup them, like Mr Brand did when he tried to catch a sunbeam. Only I'm not trying to catch any more, I'm trying to offer, like you do with a gift or a prayer.

And then it comes to me, the light, it touches me, it settles not beneath my hands, but in them. Like my hands are a nest.

35

Perhaps the breath lies in my cupped hands for just a few seconds, or maybe it's a minute, or five minutes, or even an hour. I can't say; I lose track of time. Nothing seems to matter very much any more, and I have a sense of peace and happiness and of being full up, but not full up like when you've eaten too much, just full in the way of being complete, of not needing to worry or search for anything any more.

Then, of course, there is a whoosh and a whistle and the breath flies back, as it always does, to the flask. But I am still in a slightly dreamlike state and my mind washes around until it finds something on which it can settle and that thing is names.

Lalitavajri.

Supreme Striker.

Zoe.

Jess.

Jessica.

Even though this has been my name since I was born, I've never thought about it before and I don't know what it means, so I take myself to the computer and do some Googling. The first site I try says *Jessica* means *wealthy*, which doesn't feel like me at all. But what was I expecting? What name would be right for me? *She who is alone? She who never quite seems to fit? She who makes stuff up?* Next I Google *Zoe. Zoe* is apparently Greek for *life* and that sounds a much stronger, more interesting name than mine. But then I suppose Zoe is life, she's just brimming with it, which is why I love her.

Yes, despite everything, I love her.

I move on to Richie and Clem, I can't help myself. *Richie* is the Scottish form of *Richard* and means *Ruler of Power*. Whereas *Clem* comes from *Clement* meaning *merciful, gentle*. Clem, my gentle little clam.

Then I realise what all this name stuff is actually about. The breath. Because when I look down at the pearly, pulsing thing, I think it should have a name. I think I shouldn't be calling it *Thing* or *It*, or even *The*

Breath, because it's too big and important for that. And if Lalitavajri can have a name made up for her, why can't I make one up for my breath?

No, not *my* breath. *The* breath — the biggest and smallest thing in the world.

What should you call such a breath?

And I want to call it (or is it actually him? Or her?) *Storm*, but that's too violent, doesn't describe the longing-on-the-window sill, the tender nesting. So I think of *Snuffle* and that's too small and far too like a kitten, and I begin to think this naming stuff isn't as easy as you think and no wonder my parents stopped at Jess.

Then the word *bardo* pushes itself into my mind and I start some more googling, and I get a heap of stuff I don't understand like *Simplex Physics above the Planck Energy* (which doesn't seem so simplex to me) and *octonionic spacetime* (which Si would probably understand perfectly) and also a big wiki article on the Six Bardos and other *intermediate or liminal states.*

Liminal.

What about that as a name? It doesn't sound like a boy's name, or a girl's name. And that's good. Because, if we're talking bardos, my beautiful butterfly breath seems like a bardo between genders, not exactly a girl, but not a boy either. Something that could be both perhaps – or neither. On the negative side, Liminal sounds a bit like a lemon. But it means threshold (Si would be proud of my research), and that's what I think my breath is, on the threshold of something, although I don't know what.

"How would Liminal be?" I ask the flask. "You know, as a name?"

No reply. Not even the slightest twitch or swirl or glint of a fishtail.

And I'm just about to justify my choice, start being persuasive, when I remember how I felt when Si took the flask in his hands and declared it to be an eighteenth-century whisky bottle, a pumpkin seed flask. How he tried to tack it down, see around all its corners, know what it was, only he didn't know at all.

And I think, maybe I'm just trying to do the same thing. I'm trying to know something that perhaps can't be known. And what this flask and its inhabitant needs more than anything else is just some space, some peace and quiet to be whatever – whoever – it is. Free from people like me trying to sticky tape up its throat or slap a name on its ever-changing colours.

Which is, I realise suddenly, not unlike the way I sometimes feel myself.

That sometimes I'm small and sometimes I contain mountains.

How do you put a name on that?

36

Gran calls up the stairs to say she just has to pop to the shops and will I be all right alone for a moment?

I call back yes although, of course, I will not be alone.

As soon as I hear the front door close, I take the flask downstairs and set it on the piano. Another thing I hate about the Tinkerbell piano, other than the fact that it has two non-working notes, is that it stands in the hall. Yes, the hall. I think a piano should be in a room where you can go in and close the door, where you can be all lost in that piano for a while, with nobody coming and going and nobody interrupting and nobody hearing anything you play until you're ready to play it to them.

Si, who understands many things, does not understand this.

Si says, "This space in the hall, it's a perfect piano-sized space. What are you complaining about?"

I'm complaining about them listening in. Them hearing me struggle to express whatever's going on in my heart, here in the hall. Which is why I often play when people are out. Like now.

I've been making up songs since I was about six.

"They just flow out of her," says Mum.

But actually they don't. They come very quietly and from somewhere faraway and deep, and often I don't quite hear them right at first. I have to be very quiet and still and strain to listen. Sometimes there's just a note or two, sometimes a chord, and the words, if there are words, they don't come until the tune has almost finished itself. Because it's only when the song is almost complete that I begin to know what it might be about.

Today the song, which has been whispering to me for a couple of days now, comes in small and fragile. I want to say to it, *Be brave, I'm listening for you, I'll find you,* but sometimes it doesn't work like that. Sometimes a song has to find its own bravery.

I don't know how long I sit at the piano, listening, and letting my hands wander gently, carefully over the keys. Then I hear a phrase I recognise, and I can put my fingers and my mind straight on it. But it's only when I play it out loud that I hear what it is. It's a hair from the lion's mane in Aunt Edie's song 'For Rob'. It's the smallest, tiniest thread and probably nobody would recognise it but me – but there it is right inside this new song. I listen even harder, expecting perhaps to hear other notes from 'For Rob', a spark of sky, a blade of grass, but I don't. Instead there's something else coming, something broader, richer, happier than anything in 'For Rob', and then I think perhaps it's some blossom from the cherry trees in Aunt Edie's 'Spring Garden'. Only I can't quite catch it, and the more I reach for it, the more it pulls away. I want to bring the two things together, the sadness of 'For Rob' and the other happier thing, I want to make them fit, find their harmonies. But the harder I try, the more the music resists me. The song says, *Do not summon me now, Jess, you do not know who I am.* So I go quiet and patient again, start listening, whisper back to the song: *I'll wait.*

I'll wait as long as it takes.

"Oh, good girl, Jess," Gran bundles through the front door with a bag of shopping in each hand. "I meant to tell you to get on with your practice."

Practice.

I get up and shut the lid of the piano.

37

In the evening, Mum rings. Her voice from the hospital sounds stretched thin.

"Are you all right, Jess?"

"I'm fine."

Si must have told my mother about her strange daughter and the singing flask. Can that conversation really have only been last night? It seems like a million years ago.

"I know it must be difficult for you…"

"It's fine, Mum. I'm fine."

"Sure?"

"I'm sure."

"You know I love you?"

"Yes."

"And Si loves you too."

Do I know that?

"He really does."

I say nothing.

"I'm sorry I can't come home," says Mum. "Not yet, anyway."

"It's OK. I'm fine. How are the babies?"

She lets go a little sigh. "We had some results today. Some of the tests came back."

"Yes?"

"They share a liver, Jess. Separate hearts, but only one liver." She pauses. "Do you know what that means?"

"Yes," I say. Because Si has told me. The more organs the twins share the more difficult any separation is. "Why can't they stay together?" I burst out then. "Why can't they?"

"I don't know," Mum says. "I don't know anything any more."

And then, very softly, she begins to cry.

38

Si has barely been home since I informed him he was not my parent, and when he does finally appear, he goes straight into the garage and gets out Roger the Wreck's trolley.

"I have to fix the timing chain," he announces.

It's the timing chain that drives the camshaft which, in turn, opens the valves which let the fuel mixture in and the exhaust out. I know this because, for nearly a year, Si's been talking about the function and importance of a timing chain and how this particular one could break at any time on account of The Rattle.

"Hear that rattle, Jess?"

Actually, no. Mainly because this boneshaker of a car makes so many bangs and clatters and rattles that distinguishing The Rattle from any number of other rattles is beyond me.

"It's a very distinctive sound," says Si. "Like a bike chain slipping."

And the faster the car goes, the louder the rattle.

Apparently.

Anyway, here we are on Good Friday, and Si is all overalled up with his tools laid out beside him.

"I have to fix it today," says Si.

For a whole year he hasn't fixed it.

Why now?

And then I have a totally non-scientific, non-rational thought about the timing chain. Maybe that's why it's called a timing chain, because the timing is crucial. Si has to fix the chain today otherwise… otherwise…

Otherwise what?

The monsters will get us.

Have you ever played the Pavement Crack Game? Zoe and I used to play it all the time. *If we step on a single crack between paving stones on the way to the park, the monsters will get us.* Aged five, Zoe and I knew every crack between the cul-de-sac and the swings. We never stepped on a single one, and that's how we kept safe.

I decide the broken timing chain is a crack. If we

can mend it today, Si and I, then the monsters won't come. They won't get me, and more importantly, they won't get the twins.

"Do you need some help?" I ask Si.

He stands quite still then and looks me straight in the eye and I hold his gaze. Si can talk for England, but he doesn't talk now. Which makes me want to say I'm sorry about the parent thing, but I don't know how to, so I just go to the back of the garage and find a pair of blue overalls. As I roll up the sleeves and the trouser legs, I remember how this man, who is not my father, used to lift me on to his shoulders at the end of a walk too long for my toddler legs. I remember how he was never impatient with me when, with Mum already waiting in the car, I cried for him to take me back into the house so I could check on Spike. And, speaking of monsters, I also remember how he would make sure to close the door of my wardrobe at night because he knew I feared the things which lurked there in the dark. I return to Si looking like the Michelin man. I still don't say anything to him but he speaks to me.

"Thank you, Jess," he says. "Thank you very much. I could really use some help today."

And he smiles one of those smiles like incense.

"First up, the radiator then," says Si.

He begins by loosening the radiator hoses, talking as he goes, explaining what he's doing and I'd forgotten this about his maintenance work, how very instructive it is, as though he's passing on wisdom that will, one day, allow me to construct an entire engine from scrap metal and memory alone.

I help him lift the radiator out.

"Now for the crank pulley bolts," he says. "Pass me the wrench."

And I do. Like I'm some junior doctor in an operating theatre.

Which, of course, makes me think of the twins. Although, in fact, I'm never not thinking about the twins.

"Mum told me," I say, "about the tests. About how they share a liver."

"Yes," says Si. "Not great news."

"So what do the doctors say now then?" I ask. "About the operation?"

"Depends which one you ask," says Si, as he puts metal to metal and turns. "At the last count there were about twenty-two of them."

"Twenty-two!"

"Four surgeons, four anaesthetists… Can you pass me that hammer?" I pass him the little copper mallet and he begins a soft tap tap tapping. "Remember, always go gently on a crank pulley," he says, tap tap tapping. "Although they won't all be in the operating theatre at once. They have to work in shifts… Ah, here we go." The crank pulley comes out. "Now for the timing chain cover. Ratchet please, and socket."

There are about twenty small tubular attachments in the socket tray. "What size?" I ask.

"9/16th should do it, I reckon."

I pass him the relevant socket and he screws it on to the ratchet head.

"But when are they going to do it?" I ask. "The op?"

"Not for a few months yet," says Si. His arm is deep inside the car engine. "It's safer for the babies if they can grow a bit first. Hmm. I think I'm going to have to go at this from underneath."

I get out the jack for him and wheel it under a jack point.

"Haven't forgotten everything then, have you?" says Si. And he's pleased with me, and right now, I like him being pleased with me.

He cranks the car up and then goes to fetch the trolley.

And with the trolley come the twins, of course, one underneath the car and one hopping about for a spanner.

"And what," I say, "what are their..." Only I can't finish the sentence.

"Chances?" says Si. "Good. Basically good, I think. But no one's really prepared to stick their neck out. There are so many different factors to be taken into consideration."

He slips himself under the car and I go with him, elbowing my way along the oily cardboard so I'm lying right beside him. Almost as close, I think, as Clem is to Richie. But not quite.

"If it was just their livers that were joined, that would be one thing. But it's also the lower sternum and the ribs and some part of the abdominal cavity and..." He pauses to fit the socket head over the lowest bolt.

"But the heart, they don't share a heart," I say. I hadn't realised I'd been hanging on to this fact. "That's the main thing, isn't it?"

"Well, apparently there may be a small joining of the pericardium, after all." He begins to turn the wrench. "That's the covering of the heart. And Clem's VSD doesn't help and..." He spins the ratchet. "Ow! Ow!

Jeez!" A stream of curses follows.

Instead of catching the bolt, he's caught his knuckles.

He kicks himself out from under the car, still cursing, and I elbow my way out behind him.

His knuckles are bleeding and I don't like the blood, not because my stepfather is hurting, but because the blood came when he was speaking about Clem and that brings the monsters closer. I mean, why did it have to be Clem, the weaker twin, the one who *dips* – why did it have to be Clem's name all spilt and spattered with blood?

"Half-inch," says Si, sucking at his fist. "Should have used a half-inch not a 9/16th. Idiot."

I need to do something to help. "Shall I get you a plaster?"

"Yes – over there." He nods at a cabinet at the other end of the garage, beneath the Morris Authorised Dealer sign and a bunch of red onions. "Top drawer, I think."

I find an old box with a random selection of different-sized plasters and help him patch himself up. Mum would have made him wash his hands first.

"First rule of mechanics – check your socket size. Right. Let's try again."

I hand him a half-inch socket and we both resume

162

positions underneath the car. This time the bolts come away easily.

He removes the timing chain cover and then slides out again.

"We'll do the timing marks from up top," he says. "They need to be lined up and the crank has to be at TDC," he says. "Do you remember TDC?"

"Top Dead Centre," I say.

"That's my girl!" he says.

His girl.

He works in silence for a while, but his mind, not unlike mine, remains with the twins, because then he says, "There'll be a rehearsal operation first."

"What?"

"A rehearsal. When they go through everything. Who's going to do what on the day. So, unlike us, they don't end up with the wrong-sized socket."

"But what if they do end up with something wrong?"

He pauses. "They won't. That's the point of the rehearsal." He smiles, but this time it's a little tight. "Come on now – chain tensioner."

He fiddles with something I can't see and the timing chain comes free. It looks nothing much, it looks like a slightly bigger version of a bicycle chain. Yet it can rattle and break and make the engine fail. The car remains all mixed up with Clem.

"Now all we have to do," Si says, holding the new chain, "is fit this little beauty and redo everything in reverse order."

But it doesn't happen quite that way because, when he's fitted the new chain and checked the timing marks again and refitted the tensioner, he has to turn the crankshaft two revolutions and when he does that one of the chain teeth jumps and the timing marks are out of alignment.

"Typical!" he says. He looks at his watch. "Maybe we should break," he says. "Get some lunch."

"No," I say, "we have to finish it. Get the job done. Now."

"Since when did you become chief mechanic?" he says, but he's smiling as he starts all over again.

I wonder then what will happen with the babies if something goes wrong, because an operation is not like a car, and the doctors won't just be able to start it all over again, will they?

Eventually Si gets the cover back on and checks and seals the new gasket so it doesn't leak oil. Then he reassembles the radiator. It's late, late into the afternoon now.

"Now for the moment of truth," Si says, and he starts the engine.

The car coughs and spits and rattles, and then roars into life.

"Fantastic," he says. "Listen."

I listen.

"Not a peep," he says, face beaming.

So we won this one, I think, despite the blood on Clem. We've kept the monsters at bay.

Si turns the engine off, gets out and pats the car on the bonnet. "My perfect, perfect little moggie."

39

I think about perfect.

I think about this Morris Traveller 1000, Si's little moggie, which still rattles and bangs and splutters, but is – according to its loving owner – perfect.

I think about the flask, which is slightly lopsided, the glass of one of its shoulders slightly thicker than the other. I actually go upstairs and hold it in my hand. The little seed fish (which aren't swimming today) are actually blemishes, bubbles in the glass which shouldn't really be there, mistakes in the glassmaking process. These imperfections are also the beautiful part of the flask. They are what shimmer and shine as the flask breathes, lives.

Then I think about my brothers lying together in their cot. They are not perfect, they are not even normal according to Paddy.

They're not any old twins. They're Siamese.

In the old days, before medicine could make people perfect, conjoined twins stayed the way they were born. Like Chang and Eng. Si showed me pictures of them online. Born in Thailand (or Siam, as it was then) in 1811, Chang and Eng were joined down the chest in just the same way as Richie and Clem. They began life in the circus, just like Paddy said, being exhibited as 'curiosities' all over the world. But they broke free, bought a plantation, ran their own businesses, got married to sisters and had twenty-one children between them. They were happy and lived until they were seventy-two.

No one tried to separate Chang and Eng. They were allowed to stay together.

Then I wonder – what's more perfect? Two little boys joined, or two little boys separated? And I try and imagine a world where everyone is born conjoined and only once every thousand, thousand births, do separate human beings arrive. Then I watch conjoined people bending over the separate cots and gasping. And, all at once, a team of twenty-two doctors (in eleven pairs of two) arrives to sew those little babies together again, so nobody will ever know they were born apart. And when the doctors have done their work and it's all gone swimmingly, I hear the relatives heave sighs of relief and say, "What perfect little boys."

40

While I'm on perfect, I think about Zoe. I haven't spoken to her since I discovered her name means life, since she shouted over her shoulder, *Since when were we joined at the hip?*

And she hasn't spoken to me either.

This friend I made in kindergarten. This person who bounds into my life two or three times a week and with whom I've been as close as Richie is to Clem.

I decide to ring her up, I decide to tell her about her beautiful life-giving name.

"Hello," I say brightly.

"Hi," she says, but she sounds suspicious, like I'm just about to go all heavy on her again.

So what I actually say is, "They share more organs than we thought." It just sort of falls out of me, so maybe I was always going to say this.

"What?" says Zoe.

"The twins. They share ribs and a bit of their lower sternum and their abdominal cavity and a bit of pericardium, which is the heart. Their heart."

"Oh," says Zoe.

"And also their liver. They just have the one liver."

"Urgh," she says. "That's gross."

Gross.

I put the phone down.

She rings back.

"Look," she says, "I didn't mean gross like... gross."

"What did you mean?"

"I meant, you know... Nothing against your brothers or anything. And I don't have a problem with internal organs, but livers. I mean nobody wants to talk about stuff like that, do they?"

I do. I have to, otherwise it all just sits like a heavy red stone in my brain.

"Since 1950," I say to my friend Zoe, "seventy-five per cent of separations result in one live twin." This isn't one of Si's statistics. It's one I found myself. On the net.

"Seventy-five per cent?" queries Zoe, as if she's

trying to work out the maths.

"Yes," I say. "Or, put it another way, seventy-five per cent of the time, when they separate people who have been," I pause, "so close… one twin dies."

"Oh," she says.

"So who do you think it'll be?" I ask.

"Jess…" she begins. "*Jess*…"

"Who?" I say.

"Do we have to—"

"Who?" I interrupt. "Which one?"

"Neither – probably neither. Jess – what's got into you?"

"You have to say: Richie or Clem."

Zoe or Jess?

"Why are you asking me this stuff?"

I have a vision: me on my mobile, Zoe on hers. No wire between us, but joined nonetheless, joined by some powerful but invisible signal, and if I press the red button on my phone, that signal will just snap off, snap away.

I press the red button.

There should be silence. So how come I hear the rip of a surgeon's knife?

41

The following day we go to the hospital.

"We're going to bring your mum home," says Si.

"And the babies?"

"No, not the babies. Not yet. And only Mum for the afternoon. Apparently I can't be trusted to bring in the right change of clothes."

In my pocket I have the flask. It has been quiet and almost colourless every day since I tried to paste the name *Liminal* on to it. But I'm aware of the breath, its quiet ins and outs. Sometimes I think I even hear it when I'm sleeping. Which is impossible.

Only, recently, I've begun to believe that nothing is impossible.

Si turns the radio on and we don't talk much

and eventually we arrive at the hospital and ascend fifteen floors in the lift.

In the Special Care Unit, Mum is not on a bed any more, she's sitting in a chair beside the babies. I've been doing a lot of worrying about the babies, but not about Mum. She looks drained and thin.

"Here you are," she says, and she gets up to greet me. "Missed you." She gives me a hug and I think I can feel her bones.

"Here's your big sister, boys," she says to the babies.

I look into the Perspex cot and I expect to see that the twins have grown, because babies do grow fast, everyone says so. *My, how they've grown!* But my brothers still look tiny, their heads still not filling their tiny knitted hats. I pay particular attention to Clem – is he really smaller than his brother? I don't know, maybe not, but his little hand is on Richie's shoulder, so it still looks like he's holding on.

Both babies are asleep, facing each other, their little mouths occasionally munching at precisely the same moment, as if they were having exactly the same eating dream. And then I wonder about their dreams. Do they share dreams, or do they have separate ones?

"Happy dreams," I whisper down at them. "Have

happy dreams." And they munch and their eyelids flicker too, and I suddenly feel overwhelmed with love for them.

It seems no time at all before a nurse comes to wheel them away for yet more tests.

"They'll have done so many tests before they come out of here," jokes Si, "they'll be able to go straight to university."

The nurse laughs, but Mum doesn't. She just watches the babies leave as if somebody was wheeling away her life.

"Come on now," says Si. "Let's make the most of the time."

He takes Mum's suitcase and her hand and helps her into the lift.

When we get down to ground level, and the doors swish open on to the outside world, Mum seems to stumble a little, blink in the daylight.

"Are you all right?" says Si. "Are you sure you want to make the journey? I mean, for such a short time?"

"Sure," says Mum. She nods at me. "Got to see my other baby, haven't I?"

Si helps her into the car and we begin the journey home.

"It's amazing," says Mum.

"What?" asks Si.

"The world," says Mum, as if she's been gone from it for a hundred years. "It's so bright. And big." She pauses. "And busy." Then she turns around and looks at me. "And you, Jess, even you've changed."

"Have I?"

"Yes – you've grown up a bit, I think."

And I don't know if she means *grown up – mature*, or *grown up – taller* or even just *grown up compared with the tiny, tiny twins* and I don't have time to think about this because Si butts in with: "Jess helped me with Roger the Wreck yesterday. We did the timing chain."

"The timing chain!" Mum exclaims. "So you've finally done it? Turned Roger the Wreck into, well, just Roger?"

"Well," says Si, slightly taken aback. "There's always more one can do on a moggie."

Mum laughs and touches him very lightly on the back of the neck.

And, just for a moment, everything feels all right.

42

Si asks Mum what she wants to do with her few hours at home.

"I want to eat fresh vegetables," says Mum, "and go to church."

There are very few vegetables served in the hospital, apparently, and those that are, are frozen. Mum wants to eat fresh courgettes and fresh onions and fresh tomatoes and fresh mushrooms.

"And green beans," says Mum. "I could kill for some green beans."

So Si says he will drop her at the church and go on a vegetable hunt.

"Will you come with me, Jess?" Mum asks.

Mum doesn't go to church so much for the the services, but for the candles. When we're away on holiday, she goes into every church we pass. She lights candles in memory of my father and I light them too.

"Yes," I say. "Of course."

Si drops us at St Nicholas' which is a small flint church with a square tower.

"Do you know what day it is?" she asks as we enter.

"Saturday," I say.

"Holy Saturday," she says. "The day between Good Friday and Easter Sunday. The day of Christ's entombment."

"A bardo then," I say.

"Huh?" says Mum, but she's not really listening.

We're whispering, even though there is no one in this quiet place but us. The last time I was in this church was at Christmas when it blazed with light and golden angels and dark holly and statues of the Holy Family stood in real straw. Now the church is stripped, there are no flowers, the altar is bare, the cross covered in a black cloth.

Mum takes a seat at the back of the church, as though she hasn't quite got the energy to go to the front yet, and I sit beside her. She takes a kneeler and sinks down, head in her hands. I don't know what she's praying about, but I can imagine.

I don't take a kneeler. I just sit on the hard wooden pew and look at the dense gloom in the church. I wish it was Easter Sunday, I wish someone would just roll back the rock like they did in front of Jesus' tomb and everything be light and bright again for ever.

But maybe nothing's for ever.

Zoe.

She's not for ever, she's moving on, moving away from me. And if she isn't going all of her own accord, then I'm pushing her, aren't I? I'm just putting the knife in and slamming down the phone to show her I don't care, which just shows how much I do care. Can't she see that? Then I get cross with myself for sitting in a church and thinking about Zoe when my brothers are probably dying. How can Zoe be as important as the twins? I mean, our relationship, Zoe's and mine, it's hardly life or death, is it?

But that's how it sometimes feels to me.

In fact, more than this. It feels that my join with Zoe, which, OK, didn't start at birth, but was certainly there by the time we were both four, that join, sometimes gets all muddled up in my head with the web that joins my brothers. As though what happens between me and Zoe will impact on what happens to Richie and Clem.

Yeah, right.

Mum picks herself up from her prayer, and hangs the kneeler back up.

"The Anglo-Saxons believed," she says, "that life is just the flight of a sparrow through a great lighted hall, that we come from the dark and we will return to the dark."

I don't know what this means and I don't ask her, because she looks so sad and I know that she's been to her place when kneeling, just as I've been to mine, and it's probably a private place.

We go together then towards the front of the church where there's a candle rack, four rows of little black metal dishes with black metal candle spikes in the middle, and a locked box for donations. There are normally one or two pale, thin candles burning here, but today there are none and Mum hesitates, as though maybe we shouldn't be lighting candles here on Holy Saturday, maybe we should wait until the Easter light comes in on Sunday.

But she won't be here on Easter Sunday. And there are candles waiting beneath the rack and she takes three and posts money into the box.

Three candles. She has never taken three candles before.

"First," she says, "for your father."

I hold the candle and she strikes the match.

"For Jeremy," she says, as the wick catches.

"For Dad," I say and I push the thin wax end on to the spike. You mustn't push too hard, the candles are so thin that if you do, they can split and fall.

There's a moment's silence between us and then she says that she wants to light candles for the babies. And part of me wants to stop her. I want to say: *We can't light a candle for Dad who's dead and for the babies who...*

Mum interrupts my thought. "I'll do one for Richie. Will you do Clem's?"

Which brings the monsters.

Because sometimes, when you light one candle from another, one of the flames gutters, it dies.

"Yes," I say, "I'll do it."

The Pavement Crack Game.

Mum holds Richie's candle. I hold Clem's. If either of the flames gutter...

I light mine first, from Dad's, and I do it very, very carefully and the flame leaps up. It burns strong and bright, and I let go the breath I've been holding and push the candle end very gently on to the spike.

Clem lives.

Then Mum takes Richie's candle and lights it from Clem's and it doesn't take immediately, so she pushes down a little harder and there's a sudden fizz and when she takes the candle away, Richie's candle is lit and Clem's extinguished.

Clem's candle is dead.

Clem again. Why Clem? The monsters laugh, just like they did in the garage when Clem got all spattered with Si's blood.

I hear myself gasp, but Mum just says, "Oh, bother. Let's try that again."

She places Richie's candle on the rack and relights Clem's from Dad's. It burns brightly, innocently.

"There," she says. "God bless and look after them all."

But I don't think He will.

All of a sudden, I don't think He Gives a Monkeys.

43

When we get back home, Mum organises fresh clothes for herself and Si makes some sort of ragout with the vegetables. By the time we sit down to eat it's about 3 p.m.

I sit at the table, but even though it's late, I'm not hungry – and it's not the fact that it's a plate of vegetables. I quite like vegetables. It's about what happened in the church, it's about playing the Pavement Crack Game and losing.

"I'm not hungry," I say.

"Eat," says Si.

So I do. It feels like a kind of giving-in. Afterwards, while Mum and I wash up, Si goes off in the car to get more petrol for the return journey to the hospital.

Mum has been home less than three hours and soon she will be gone again, who knows for how long.

"Mum…" I say.

"Yes, Jess?"

"Do you know anyone in Aunt Edie's life called Rob?"

"Rob?" says Mum. "Rob who?"

So I tell her about Aunt Edie's music 'For Rob'.

"Must have been someone really important," I say.

"How do you know that?"

"Because of the music. Because of what she wrote."

Mum pauses. "No, sorry, doesn't mean anything to me. Why don't you ask Gran?"

And I say I will, but I won't, of course, because whatever Gran knows, she's not telling.

There's a silence and then Mum says, "Do you want to know why I really came home today, Jess?"

"Vegetables?" I offer.

Mum laughs. "Of course not. And not for the church or the clothes either. I came home to see you."

"I know. You said."

"Did I?" She looks at me quizzically.

"At the hospital."

"Yes. I suppose I did. But no one but you would have noticed, Jess. You're a really special person, you know that?"

I shrug.

183

"And sensitive. And sometimes…"

I wait.

"Sometimes I'm a bit like that too. I can tell what people are saying when they're not saying things."

This would be a muddle in anyone else's mouth, but I know exactly what Mum means.

"What am I not saying?" I ask.

Mum puts her head on one side. "You tell me."

So many things. Where to begin? The flask, the worry about the babies, the Pavement Crack Game, the monsters coming closer. Zoe.

Zoe.

Zoe.

"Zoe," I say.

"Go on," says Mum.

Then I think maybe Si hasn't gone to get petrol (why couldn't he get petrol on the journey back?). I think he's gone to give Mum and me Some Space.

"I don't think Zoe likes me any more."

"Oh? And why do you say that?"

I don't tell her it might be because I shouted at her about livers and slammed the phone down on her, deliberately cutting the cord between us. I say, "I think she'd rather be with Paddy."

Mum takes my hand and I let her. "People can like more than one person at a time, you know," she says. "Like just because I have two more children now, doesn't mean I love you any less, Jess. Not at all."

Ha. I bet she's glad she's had an opportunity to work that into the conversation. Still – I like hearing it. It gives me the same sort of feeling I had when I was tiny and had a fever and she put a cool hand on my forehead.

"Human beings," she continues, "they – we – have an infinite capacity for love."

"But Zoe," I begin again, "she used to come here all the time. Come around. Bound straight in. Barely knocked. You'd have thought she lived here. And now," I pause lamely, "she doesn't."

Mum takes a breath and I prepare myself for Something Adult.

"Jess," she says, "you and Zoe may just be growing apart. You've known her since you were in kindergarten. When people get older, they find different parts of themselves. What used to be a good fit, might not be such a good fit as you grow up, develop your interests. Find out who you really are." She pauses. "And that's OK, Jess."

"It's not OK," I say solidly.

"I don't mean it doesn't hurt, it can leave a hole…"

A hole?

"But in that space," continues Mum, "new things can come, new friends."

But I don't want any new friends. I just want Zoe, my mirror image, my better, bolder other half. And suddenly Zoe seems to me like Richie, she seems zesty big. And I'm the smaller, weaker twin; I'm Clem, clinging to her for dear life.

"Why do they have to cut them apart?" I exclaim then. "Why can't they just let the twins stay together for ever and ever?"

Mum raises an eyebrow. "Maybe they'll have a better life apart."

"They won't," I cry.

Mum still has my hands in hers. Very gently she begins to stroke my fingers. "Maybe together…" she says, "maybe together…" she repeats, "they might just… suffocate each other."

44

This is what usually happens on my Easter Day. In the morning, Mum makes me an Easter nest. The nest always contains one large hollow chocolate egg, numerous loose tiny sugar-coated speckled ones, a couple of chocolate ducks in golden foil and – sometimes – a box of flat little bunnies eating flat chocolate carrots. Mum puts all the goodies into a plastic bag and then hides them: they might be buried in the ironing pile, hung behind a coat in the front porch, locked in the Christmas trunk.

"She's a bit old for an Easter nest, isn't she?" Si said last year.

And the previous year.

And the year before that.

But the nest still comes. Except this year Si has driven

Mum back to the hospital so there is no nest. Plonked in the middle of the kitchen table is an oversized chocolate rabbit. Not hidden at all.

"Happy Easter," Gran says.

In the afternoon of an Easter Sunday, at four o'clock precisely, teatime, Zoe always comes. She even knocks on the door, so I actually have to open it to her.

"Surprise," she says.

Only it isn't, because she's come every year since her mum brought her when she was four. She brings what she brought that first ever time – a Cadbury's creme egg – and she says what she said that first ever time: *I gots it for you special*. And I say, *Specialsmeschal* (I don't really know why I say that) and then, in return, I give her a Kinder Egg with the orange-and-white foil wrapping and the little plastic toy inside and she says: *Specialsmeschal*, and then we hug and laugh and eat the chocolate and make the stupid toy (it's usually a tank), but of course it isn't about the chocolate or the toy and we both know that.

I start clock-watching at 3 p.m. The second hand of the kitchen clock ticks impossibly slowly. Every minute takes approximately two weeks. I listen for the sound of footsteps (running, bounding, enthusiastic footsteps) in the cul-de-sac. There aren't any, but I tell myself that

that's because it's early, three-quarters of an hour early, half an hour early, ten minutes early. I don't go to look out of the window, not even at four o'clock. Not at 4.05. Or 4.10. Or 4.15. At 4.20 I accept it's over. Our friendship. It really is. And it doesn't matter how long I sit stubbornly watching the clock (I'm still there at half-past five), it won't make any difference.

I can feel the Kinder Egg in my pocket going all hot and sweaty, probably because I keep touching it, I keep squishing at it, to check it's still there, to check I've kept my part of the bargain. By six o'clock the egg is mainly mush.

Gran watches me watching the clock.

"What's going on?" she says.

"Zoe didn't come," I say.

"It's Easter," says Gran. "Why would she?"

"She always comes on Easter Sunday."

"Probably got family over," says Gran. "Or gone out somewhere. Maybe she'll come later."

But she won't. I know she won't. The only time her family ever went away for Easter she told me, told me weeks in advance.

"You could always ring her," says Gran.

But I'd just hear the rip of the surgeon's knife again.

45

When I wake the following day, there is a light frost on the windowpane and everything in the world seems colder. There is no news from the hospital.

"No news is good news," says Gran.

There is no news from Zoe.

Which is not good news.

The breath is on the window sill, looking out.

"What do you want? What are you waiting for?"

No reply.

Everything seems suspended, waiting.

"Haven't you got anything to do?" asks Gran.

"Yes," I say. "I have."

I go to the local shop and buy a new Kinder Egg. The sight of the white-and-orange foil brings a lump to my throat. Why is it always Zoe's responsibility to come to my house? Overnight, I have re-examined my friendship. I have noticed that, for years and years, Zoe has been the visitor and I have been the visited.

Why?

Am I some queen that it's me who sits in state to receive her? Or is it just that she's so full of life – so full of Zoe – that she's made all the running, and I've just stood by, watching? Waiting. What's wrong with me? Friendship is a two-way street – or it should be. I have decided that I will go to Zoe's house and give her my small gift.

Zoe's car is in her drive, the family is at home. I go up to the front door, press the bell and listen to the two-tone ring.

Ding-dong.

Like my heart.

Ding-dong. Ding-dong. Ding-dong.

Someone comes to the door, I see the shadow on the other side of the glass, they pause to peek through the spyhole. I half-hope it's Zoe's mother, she'll greet me with a smile.

It isn't Zoe's mother. It's Zoe.

"Hi," she says, not aggressive, but not really friendly either, somewhere between wary and neutral. It makes me feel confused, as if whatever I say it isn't going to be the right thing. So I say nothing.

"You all right?" she says. She keeps the door not quite open far enough for me to come in. So, of course, I don't go in. I stand in my big silence. If it were her at my door, she'd just bound in.

"Happy Easter," I say at last. It doesn't sound that happy, but it doesn't sound ironic either.

"Sorry about yesterday…" she begins.

"Doesn't matter at all," I say, far too fast. "I'm sorry about the phone thing."

"Hmm," she says.

I go on standing.

"I was going to come around yesterday," she adds, "only…" She trails off.

"Doesn't matter," I say again, as if that will make it more likely. "We were busy too." I try a little smile.

She shrugs, embarrassed.

"Zoe?"

"Yes?"

I'm getting an idea; it's coming in very sudden and important. "I want you to do something, do something for me. Will you, Zoe? Please." There's a certain desperation in my voice.

"What?" she says, curious but flat.

"I want to go to the Buddhist Centre again," I tell her. "I want to go there with you."

"Huh?"

"Do a meditation like Lalitavajri offered."

"Why?"

Because things melt away in that Shrine Room, I think. Because it's a place where you seem to be able to say things without words, where there are smiles like incense, where my friend Zoe looked at me with hope and longing and I swore never to let that friendship die.

"Please, Zoe," I say.

"Well…"

"It's Tuesday. It's always Tuesday. That's what Lalitavajri said. Tomorrow. Come with me, Zoe."

"Sorry," says Zoe. "I can't."

Can't or won't?

"I'm busy." She shrugs.

I shouldn't push it, I should leave it right there, but I plough on through the humiliation. "Oh – doing something nice?"

"Cinema. We're going to a film. It's all arranged."

And I don't ask her who the we is because I already know.

Her.

And Paddy.

"Right. OK, see you some other time then."

When I arrive home, I realise the Kinder Egg is still in my pocket. As for the hole Mum talked about – it's now a chasm.

46

In the night I dream about the Shrine Room. Across the golden belly of the Buddha there are little seed fish. When the Buddha breathes, the seed fish swim. I wake with a stubborn golden hope inside me. At least I still have the flask.

I take it out.

"I promised you, didn't I?"

No reply.

Bit like Zoe.

To Gran I say, "We have to go back to the Buddhist Centre. You know, for the project. Zo's… um, having her hair cut first, so she'll meet us there. Can you take me for eleven-thirty?"

Gran huffs and puffs, but as it's school work, she has to agree. I make sure we arrive early.

"Zoe will be here in a jiff, you can leave me, it's fine."

So Gran leaves me.

As I put my shoes on the rack in the porch and head up alone to the top floor, I wonder what I really hope to find here.

I want the Shrine Room to be just as I remember it, but it isn't. The previously spacious, empty floor is laid with neat rows of maroon mats, each with two small pouffe-like blue cushions. Through the skylight there's no blue sky, no scudding clouds, only a uniform grey coldness. In front of the Buddha there is no eucalyptus. There are other flowers, but I wanted there to be eucalyptus and there isn't.

I hesitate and Lalitavajri, who is rearranging some candles, turns and sees me. At once she leaves what's she's doing and comes towards me.

"It's Jess, isn't it?" she says.

"Yes." I feel surprisingly shy.

"Have you come alone?"

"No," I say, because the flask is snug in my pocket. And then, seeing her scan the room, I realise what I've said so I add, "You're here."

She smiles. "You're a very thoughtful person, aren't you, Jess?"

I'm surprised at this. I'm always surprised when people notice me.

Then she tells me to take a mat and make myself comfortable and not to worry that it's my first time. I see how other people are sitting or kneeling on the little blue cushions and I kneel like that too.

Then, keeping very still (and I wonder suddenly if Zoe could be this still), I cup my hands in front of me. I make a little nest in case the breath wants to be with me in this place.

"You'll be safe here," I whisper.

Lalitavajri goes to sit at the front of the room beside a golden bowl with a golden hammer. A few minutes later the whole room is full, maybe twenty or thirty people silently coming to sit or kneel on their cushions.

Lalitavajri welcomes us all and then, in a soft, slow voice, she asks us all to be aware of our bodies, to feel the weight of them from the ground up.

"Imagine," she says, "awareness filling your body, like soft, warm light, penetrating your bones, your muscles."

Already my eyes are closed, I've shut them instinctively. I just want to be all wrapped up alone with the words which seem like spells.

"Listen to the breath, the rising and the falling."

And I do listen to my breath and I feel the movement of my ribcage, just as Lalitavajri says. And then, in my hands, I suddenly feel it there too. The fluttering of a butterfly wing.

It has come.

"Imagine where your heart is. Make a space around your heart."

But I think there's a space around my heart already.

"The *metta bhavana*," Lalitavajri is saying now, "for those of you who are new here today, is about universal loving kindness. And loving kindness starts with ourselves. To love others, we must first love ourselves. So I ask you to wish yourself well. Say, 'May I care for myself.'"

This feels strange to me, and slightly selfish, so I can't quite say the words even inside the quietness of my head.

"Now, think of a close friend," continues Lalitavajri. "Wish them well, hope for their happiness."

I wish she'd said not *friend* but *relative*, because I want to wish the babies well, I want them to have all the love in the world. But she said *friend*, so it's Zoe who comes into my mind, Zoe dancing in the park and lying in the half-moon swing with me and looking at the sky. Only Zoe will probably never come with me to the park again.

So I haven't chosen anyone before Lalitavajri goes on. "Now, keeping yourself relaxed and open, hearing your own breath, turn your attention to a difficult person, an enemy."

And just before I tell myself I have no enemies, Zoe's face comes again. Zoe telling Paddy mumbo jumbo about the twins, Zoe shutting me out with movies, Zoe saying, *Since when were we joined at the hip?* Zoe failing to come to my house on Easter Sunday with a small creme egg. Zoe going to the movies. With Paddy.

"And noticing any resistance," says Lalitavajri, "and not judging it, imagine this person well and happy."

I notice the resistance. I notice that my bones aren't made of light any more. They're made of glass.

And I want to wish Zoe well, but right now I just can't.

Can't.

Can't.

I'm too busy.

"Now," says Lalitavajri, "move your metta, your loving kindness outwards. Let it take in everyone in this room and everyone in this town, everyone in this country, all those awake and all those asleep…"

And I see where she's going with this and I want to follow, I want to expand outward and embrace the whole world with my calm, warm bones of light. But if your bones are made of glass, you can't do that. You're all hard and fragile and have no give in you at all.

"Let your loving kindness," says Lalitavajri, "flow over all those on islands and those on continents, on babies being born and people dying…"

But nothing flows out of me except this one thought: Why has Lalitavajri yoked these babies and these dead people together? And why is she talking about babies and death at the precise moment when I'm thinking about the death of my friendship with Zoe? As if she knows something, if she knows what I know, that they're interconnected, that if one dies the other dies. Make her stop talking about babies and death! Then I think maybe it's me that's joining everything so bitterly together, me sitting here all crunched up with my mouthful of glass.

And I realise there's no space around my heart any more. It's all gone very tight. Just like my hands. My hands are clenching so tight there is no nest any more.

I've crushed it, crushed it to nothing.
So what's happened to the breath?

47

It's back in the flask. It looks weak, feeble. My mind was so full of hate I didn't notice how I squeezed it out and now it lies shivering and defeated right at the bottom of the glass. It reminds me of the candle in the church, how the flame guttered just before it died.

So I know something bad's happened even before Gran's car arrives. Before I see her face – grey and panicked.

"It's Clem," I say, as I climb into the front seat beside her. "It's Clem, isn't it?"

"How do you know?" she says. "How can you know that!"

"Your face," I lie.

"He's taken another dip," Gran says.

She makes no attempt to stall, to hide things. So it

must be worse than I thought. It must be terrible.

"What does it mean?" I can hear my voice all high and tight.

"They're going to have to bring the operation forward."

"To when?"

"Tomorrow."

"Tomorrow!"

"Yes."

"But what about the rehearsal, the practice op, where...?" Where they learn how not to pick the wrong socket spanner.

"There isn't going to be time for that," says Gran.

48

Of course, I blame myself, for all that absence of metta. What if I'd have loved everyone, loved Zoe, kept myself warm and open? It wouldn't have happened, would it? It's all my fault.

"I'm sorry," I say. "I'm really sorry."

No reply.

"Why don't you scream at me? Yell?"

Silence.

"Why don't you howl? What's happened to your big black howls?"

I'd prefer the black howls, horrible as they were, anything would be better than this shivering, dying, guttering, nearly ended flame.

I remember how I held the howling black flask close to my body and how I rocked and gave it warmth and it seemed to make a difference. I hold the flask close again, glass to skin. It makes no difference at all.

It just feels cold.

I feel cold.

Really cold.

How can you have a cold flame?

Because the flame is dying.

"Do you think Rob would want you to be behaving like this?" I shout at the flask.

No reply.

"And who is Rob, anyway?"

No reply.

Everything is colder. I don't know if it's my head, my heart or the weather.

I find myself at the piano. What's happened to my new song with the lion thread? I haven't heard a single note of it for days. Maybe I haven't been listening properly, or maybe everything that's been going on with the babies and Zoe and the hate has blocked my ears.

I put my hands on the keys, but my fingers are frozen, there is no more music in them than there is in my head. You cannot force a song, it comes in when it's ready. Surely I, of all people, know that?

I shut the lid of the piano.

One long night before the twins' operation.

How will I be able to sleep?

"Here," says Gran. "I've made you some hot milk."

I watch the hot milk going cold, just like everything else.

"Get into bed," says Gran.

I get into bed holding the flask. I think perhaps I shouldn't take my eyes off it for a second. But then there's never anything new to see, only the cold, hopeless, guttering thing.

"Why don't you make the seed fish swim?" I cry. "Just one. For me. So I know you're still there. So I know Clem's still there. Please. Please!"

No reply.

No reply!

"I hate you, hate you, hate you."

But actually it's me I hate. Because no matter how many times I go over it in my head, try to convince myself that it could just be a *coincidence*, that this new dip has nothing to do with me the way the first howling dip had nothing to do with me, I can't let myself off the hook. I'd never heard of the word *metta* before this afternoon, now it seems the only thing that matters.

Loving kindness. I mean, if you have a row with a friend, you think it's just to do with the two of you, don't you? But what if (I'm thinking this looking at the guttering flame), when any one of us is angry or hurt, then the whole sum of human happiness goes down? What then? If we're all connected, all in this together (which is, I think, what Lalitavajri was saying), then how we behave every minute of every day – that must matter too.

This is a late-night conversation I'm having with myself, and I know I'm tired and I might not be thinking too straight, but the bottom line is this: to help Clem, I feel I have to do something about the way things are with me and Zoe.

Right Now.

Then I remember that I did try – I went to her house, right? And she brushed me off. No, no, she just said she was busy and…

Think metta. Think loving kindness. Try again. Never give up.

An idea comes to me. I get out of bed, pull my dressing gown about me, and because I'm still shivering, add my duvet and go to sit at the desk.

The bureau.

The place where Aunt Edie sat writing her private letters, letters from her secret heart. I fold down the desk lid and find some paper and a black ballpoint pen. Letters, I think, are not like texts – *soz. SOZ cll me* – which can be brushed aside like flies. They're more than that, deeper. You can say things in a letter that sometimes you can't say face to face.

But what should I say?

Dear Zoe, I write.

Dear, dear, dearest Zoe.

Please feel free to go to a film with anyone you like. Not that you need my permission. You don't, of course. You're a free agent, you just do whatever you want, with whoever you want, whenever you want…

I break off. I'm laying it on too thick, making it sound as if she's doing all the taking and I'm doing all the giving. I screw the paper up, start again.

Dear Zoe,

You're wonderful. You're amazing. I love everything about you. I think I even loved you when you were four and wore that stupid vest with the pink rose on it. Wore it over the top of your jumper! So bold, so funny. Did I ever tell you that I asked my mum for a vest with a rose on? And she bought me one. Though I only ever wore mine under my jumper…

I stop again. I don't care whether you come or not. Just don't *get heavy with me.* This is heavy, isn't it? This is pressure too, this says: you have to love me as much as I love you; you have to remember how frail I am compared with you; you need to protect me. Pressure, pressure, pressure. Heavy, heavy, heavy. Sad, sad, sad. Did Aunt Edie have this trouble with her letters? I screw up a second piece of paper.

Dear Zoe, I begin for the third time. Beside me on the desk, the flame in the flask is still guttering.

I'm sorry. Sometimes my heart's all in a mess. Sometimes I say the wrong things. Want the wrong things.

Forgive me?

Love you.

Jess.

Then I add some kisses.

xxxxxxxxxx

I notice how the kisses look like a daisy chain and think that maybe this is the right letter to send, or at least a good-enough letter, so I fold it in three and sticky tape it down (as I don't have any envelopes) and write her name in bold on the front.

ZOE.

Life.

I look at the flask again. Still guttering. I wrote the

letter to change things with the flask and it hasn't. But it has changed something in me.

I feel lighter, more positive.

I rearrange the duvet from clothing to bedcover and climb into bed.

In the morning I will post this letter in at Zoe's door. I won't ring the doorbell, I won't make a big deal about it, she'll just find it when she finds it. I am calmer now, as you are when you stop shouting and begin to do something about a problem. I hold the flask close for a moment.

"You'll be all right," I whisper. "You'll see. I'll find a way. You'll be all right."

Then I sleep.

49

I wake with a start, a muscle in my leg spasming. I kick out, knock the flask (which is somehow still in my hands), grab it back, look. No change. The flame fluttering – weak and low.

Then I wonder how, in the dark of night, I can see the flask so clearly? Which is when I realise it's not dark at all. My room is full of strange white light. It's also very quiet, like someone threw a blanket over the whole world. I get up. As I peel back the duvet, I feel goosebumps flash up my arm. By the time I get to the window, I'm hugging myself, arms clasped tight, for warmth, for security. Then through the crack in the curtains I see it.

It's snowing.

The huge hush is four or five inches of snow. I

unclasp my arms and open the curtains wide. The sight is astonishing. Snow – at Easter! The world I see from my window is not the one I went to bed with. The snow covers everything: cars and houses and trees so that the view is just one landscape of white – everything joined – yes everything joined up together, because of the snow.

"Is this it? The next part of the journey?"

No reply.

I'm going to go out in the snow, although it's deep in the middle of the night. I can't not be part of this world where white earth meets white sky. I dress as quickly and as quietly as I can, tuck the flask, and also the letter, into my pocket and tiptoe downstairs.

I'm glad that I'm so practised with cracks and creaks and floorboards; waking Gran is not part of my plan. I take gloves and a scarf from the chest in the hall and my coat and wellingtons from the porch. What to do about a door key? There are keys in the kitchen, but the kitchen is directly under Gran's bedroom. I decide just to leave the door on the latch.

Then I step out into the joined-up world.

The sky is white-blue, in some places completely white, as white as the earth, which is why it's so bright, why there seems to be hardly any darkness at all. The snow itself has eased, it is very light now, just a few flurries, though it must have been snowing really heavily for hours.

The hush is extraordinary, nothing seems to be moving except for me, so I hear every sound I make as though it is amplified a thousand times. The crunch of my own footsteps in the deep new snow, and the in-out of my own breath which crystallises in a small cloud of warmth in front of my chill mouth.

I see how deep my feet go, maybe it's not four or five inches, maybe it's only three or four, but seeing my footprints, where there are no others, makes them seem significant. The map of my journey.

All along the cul-de-sac are street lights that look very orange against the white white snow. It's only a matter of moments before I arrive at Zoe's house, me the midnight postman. I think of her tucked up in bed knowing nothing about what's going on in this bright new world, but she will know. I watch my prints come up to her door. Her letter box is the low sort, so I have to kneel to push the letter in.

As I stand up again, I imagine her coming (bounding) downstairs in the morning, all excited about the snow, picking up the envelope, reading what I've written and just smiling, smiling at the world, at the words, at me. She has such a beautiful smile.

I trot happily back down her path, thinking how even my footprints have joined me to her, my house to hers.

I don't go home. I have a second mission. I'm so wrapped up in my head that I almost fail to notice there's someone else out in this night. Several doors down from Zoe's there's a young man I don't recognise heaping snow outside his garage, shaping it into something, moulding it. I don't want him to see me, I don't want him to stop me, or chat, or ask me where I'm going, because I realise I don't really want anyone in this world but me. I want it all for myself for a little while longer.

But he's too absorbed to notice anything, his head (rather like mine) is right inside whatever he is doing outside the garage in our joined-up cul-de-sac. So he lets me be and I let him be as I walk on, on towards the park.

The street lights stop here, so it is a little darker, but not much. I pass some kind of large electricity junction box, which I must have passed a million times before and never noticed. I notice it now because, in the giant hush, it is humming.

The park is a winter wonderland, better than any Christmas card I've ever seen, the trees dark shapes beneath their glittering coats of white, the odd winter pansy, yellow and purple, pushing its velvety head through the blanket of snow. I feel full of joy, as though I could run and laugh, but I don't. I keep very quiet and still, at one with the landscape.

I pass the playground, looking at the ledges of snow on the swings and slide, and on the half-moon place where Zoe and I have talked so many times, and on again to the bowling green, where the old men and the old women come out in the summer and play together with whispers and the soft clack of balls. The path to the bowling green is lit, though I've never noticed these lamps before. They are not lozenge shaped, like the street lights, but round like little yellow globes, like little worlds all of their own.

Why have I chosen the bowling green?

Because it's gated off. Because the bench I have in mind is screened from the rest of the park. It is not a place you just pass, you have to choose to go there, go deliberately.

I open the gate. *No Dogs*, it says. *No Ball Games*.

I go straight to the bench and sweep all the snow

from the left end of the bench towards the middle. I hear a rustling, which surprises me and I look up and the plant that screens the bowling green from the road turns out to be a palm tree. Or maybe not a palm tree (because how can there be a palm tree here?), but certainly a tree with long, spiky fronds which looks as if it belongs in warmer climes. The wind is rustling through the spikes, shivering them.

Next I sweep all the snow from the right-hand side of the bench towards the middle. Now I have two mounds of snow, very little mounds, but the babies are very little, so it doesn't matter. The two piles seem to be leaning towards each other. I start sculpting little arms and little hands, and bring the mounds closer in together so the space between the two gets smaller and smaller and then, all at once, there is no space between the mounds. The babies are joined.

Then I start on the heads, only there really isn't quite enough snow, so I have to pick up some from the green itself, and I forget that there is a ditch all around the bowling area, and I nearly fall, but I don't quite and that feels good. I only take as much snow as fits into my cupped hands.

I begin with Richie's head, because Richie always

seems to come first, and I take time to make Richie's head strong and stable. Then I cup my hands once again and I take snow for Clem. I don't intend to take less snow for him, but when I join the ball of snow to his chest it seems as if his head is smaller than Richie's. It is also not so stable. I press it in around the neck, but still the head wobbles, leans, seems to want to rest against his brother. I try to separate the heads.

Joined chest, separate heads.

But Clem resists me, he wants to lean against his brother. He's only happy, only stable when their heads are touching, kissing. I think, fleetingly, how it would be if my head was leaning on Zoe's shoulder, if she was supporting me.

So I let Clem be, let Richie support him.

Clem's choice.

How many other choices does my little brother have right now?

Then I stand back, look at the snow babies clinging there together, and finally pull the flask from my pocket. What am I expecting? A sign, I suppose. I'm hoping that the little flame will be just slightly stronger, slightly brighter. What I'm not expecting is what I find: a globe of shining white. The surface of the glass dense

but sparkling, like a frosted windowpane and inside…
oh, inside. How can I describe it? It's lit and fluttering
and it looks like there are strips of paper floating there,
thin pale strips, the colour paper would be if you could
cut it from moonlight. It's ghostly and beautiful and it
makes me happier than I can say because I know where
it belongs. It belongs at the heart of the snow babies.

So I put it there, lean it just where the babies join,
so that they can share. As the flask shimmers between
them, I half-expect it to act like a real heart, and for the
babies to get up off the bench and walk and dance and
fly like they did in the Snowman film Zoe and I used to
watch when we were five.

They don't, of course. It's just my heart lifting,
because I've finally made a difference. Posting the letter,
building the snow babies; one or the other, both, I don't
know. But, instead of destroying something, crushing
something up, as I did in the Shrine Room, I've begun
to build, to create, add to the sum of human happiness.

"Is that it?"

No reply.

Then, as I gaze, the flask tips slightly, responding to
some unevenness in my packing of the snow probably,
but it comes to rest more on Clem's side, just under his

arms, as though he was reaching for the flask, wanting it nearer. In this night of messages what can this be but a message?

"You want Clem? Clem wants you?"

No reply.

"Then I'll take you. I'll take you to the hospital. After the op – yes?"

After the op. What if there is no *after the op?*

What if, because there's no time for the rehearsal op, they choose the wrong socket spanner and Clem doesn't make it, he dies on the operating table?

This is a night for bravery, but suddenly I don't feel at all brave, I feel the monsters begin to crowd around again.

So I hedge my bets. I can't stop myself, I play the Pavement Crack Game one final time.

To date, the monsters and I are running even. Si and I won (just) with the timing chain. The monsters won in the church. This will be the decider.

"Winner takes all," I say. "Yes?"

No reply.

Not from the flask.

Not from the monsters.

"If the snow babies still exist when the op starts

tomorrow morning, then everything will be all right."

The op is scheduled for 8 a.m. I don't know what the time is now (the bowling green clock says 3.30, but it's been saying that ever since I arrived). Whatever time it is, the snow babies only have to last perhaps four or five hours, and it's cold and there's no one in the park, and anyway they're hidden and even the early sledgers won't come here because the bowling green area is so flat and… Surely I can win this one? Dead cert – yes?

"If the snow babies exist when the op starts," I repeat, "Richie will live. Clem will live. Both of them. They'll both survive." Then, like chucking salt over your shoulder for good luck, I add, "As will my friendship with Zoe."

Out in the moonlight, where the white sky touches the white earth, dreams feel real.

50

The wet of the snow has penetrated my gloves and my fingers are freezing. I didn't notice this before, but I'm noticing it now, just as I'm noticing how the white-blue sky has gone slightly rose-coloured and grey. Maybe it's dawn already. Only three hours for the snow babies to last. I listen for the birds, but I don't hear any. Maybe the birds are hiding. Maybe the hush has got them too. There aren't even any cars. There's just me and my breathing again and a sudden desire to be home, to be tucked up in bed.

I feel exhausted.

I say goodbye to the babies, tuck the flask back into my pocket and follow my own prints out of the park, messing them up slightly by the entrance to the bowling green, as if I could disguise my going there.

As I enter the cul-de-sac, I see that my neighbour, the other night sculptor, has mounded his snow into a huge snow mermaid, a beautiful woman who seems to be compacted together, carved out of ice. I stop to admire her. The boy (or man) is no longer there, but he's signed his name on the sculpture, as if it was a work of art: Bruno Teisler, it says. And I wonder briefly about this Bruno Teisler who lives in my close, who I've never seen before and then I pass on by, stopping only to glance up at Zoe's window, before arriving at my own house.

The light is on in our porch. The door is not closed quietly on the latch. It's wide open. And in that lighted doorway, coat and gloves on, is Gran.

51

"Where on earth have you been? Just what do you think you're doing? Don't you think I've enough to be worrying about without this, you selfish, selfish child."

These are just some of the things Gran says, or rather she shouts. She is shouting so loudly I think the whole street, the whole world will hear her. There will never be hush again.

"And you're shivering. Look at you! LOOK AT YOU! And wet. You're wet. Jess, you'll be ill. You'll be really ill. You know that?"

I don't know anything. I just feel tired and silent.

"Well, what have you got to say for yourself?"

Then she scoops me up and hugs me tighter than I've ever been hugged before, and just for once, I don't mind being all crushed up against her.

She brings me in and strips me down and makes me drink hot cocoa (I am shivering even with my hands around the warm mug). And she never stops talking and I still don't say anything.

"How could you?" she repeats, over and over. "How could you? You know about your father, don't you?"

And of course I know, but it doesn't stop her telling me again anyway.

"He went out," Gran says. "Went out in the snow when he was six. Not at night, of course. Not at night. Even he wasn't that stupid. No, in the day. He was supposed to be in the garden, playing. Children do play in the snow. For hours. And I was getting on with something in the house, like you do, and suddenly it was six o'clock. So I called for him. Called and called, only he didn't answer. So I went out. And that's when I found him. Lying flat out in the snow. Flat on his back. I thought he was dead. But he was just asleep. Asleep. How could anyone – ANYONE – just fall asleep in the snow? I'll never understand that as long as I live. Never."

There are tears in her eyes.

"And that's why he always had such a weak chest. He was a sickly boy after that. And I always wonder, when he died so young, I always wondered: if I'd looked out that afternoon, if I'd seen him, if I'd stopped him…"

I've heard this story many times and it always ends here, with the blame. But now, for the first time, I wonder too. I wonder why my father lay down in the snow to sleep. It can't have been because he was tired. There are many more comfortable places to sleep than the snow. So perhaps, like me, he was trying things out, experimenting, playing a Pavement Crack Game all of his own. If I lie down in this snow and no one finds me then…

The monsters won't get me.

I so much wish I could know that game and the boy who played it. The boy who grew up to be my father. Perhaps he would have things to teach me about monsters. And then, suddenly, I experience the loss of my father as a physical thing, an emptiness somewhere deep inside me. And I want to fill that hole with the sound of his voice; I want to hear my father talking, I could listen to him for a lifetime.

But there's only Gran talking.

52

When Gran finally finishes, she fusses me into bed.

"And don't think you're going out anywhere tomorrow!" is her parting shot. As she closes the door, I reach into my pocket.

The flask is still white, though not quite as sparkling, not on the surface anyhow. But inside, among the floating paper strips of moonlight there's something new, a thread of yellow. Or gold, pale gold, like a hair from the mane of a lion, or the brightness of a smile. It throws a filament of light to the white swirling surface, where a single seed fish swims.

"Thank you," I whisper. "Oh, thank you, thank you, thank you."

I lie down and sleep. I dream that I am lying in the snow next to my father and we keep each other warm.

53

I wake to find the flask still in my hand. I can't have let it go all night. The glass has taken heat from my body and it's warm too, its surface not frosted any more but transparent. I can clearly see the strips of moonlight, the threads of gold, and yes, the seed fish, the seed fish is still swimming.

The snow babies must have made it through the night!

So the real babies will make it through the op.

Clem will live!

Richie will live!

Zoe will smile on the world and on me!

I pull my alarm clock close. It's ten o'clock already. The babies will have been in the operating theatre for two hours. I charge downstairs in my dressing gown and arrive in the kitchen just as the phone rings. I get to it before Gran.

It's Si.

"They're OK?" I cry. "Aren't they? Richie's OK and Clem's OK and it's all going fine, even though there hasn't been a rehearsal op. Right?"

"Not exactly," says Si.

"What?"

"The op. It's been delayed."

A sudden chill. "Why?"

"The snow. Half the team haven't managed to get in. One of the doctors is marooned somewhere way out of town. Dug his car out, but the roads are impassable."

"But they're going to do it later?" I say. "As soon as everyone's there?"

"No," says Si. "They're going to delay it. They have to have everyone and they have to start on time. Can't start late and work through the night. It's a long, long process, Jess."

"But what about Clem?" I burst out.

"He's stabilised, much to everyone's astonishment. Didn't I say that? That's the good news, Jess."

Of course he has, because of the building, because of not destroying but... but...

"When's it going to be – the op – when's it going to be?"

"Tomorrow," says Si. "We hope."

"The snow babies!" I cry.

"What?" says Si.

"The snow babies have to last another twenty-four hours!"

"What are you talking about?" says Si.

54

I'm talking about marching straight to the park and standing over the snow babies with Si's large socket spanner. If anyone comes within a foot of them...

But what if they just melt? What if the God that let Clem's candle gutter in the church just parts the cloud and the sun comes out? What then? I rush to the window. No sign of a thaw. On our garden table the snow is still piled four inches deep at least. And it's cold, bitingly cold. Even Gran, who likes to tell you that she was a War Baby, and War Babies know about hardship, is standing next to the cooker with a gas ring lit to provide the warmth that the central heating seems to be struggling to achieve.

I go straight upstairs and get dressed so fast I forget the flask. I don't put on my shoes because I'm going to be wearing wellington boots, and I'm down in the porch in less than two minutes.

But so is Gran.

"And what exactly do you think you're doing?"

"I'm going out." I just have to be there, with the snow babies. That's all there is to it. I will defend them to the death.

To the life.

"Have you gone mad?"

Yes. I think so.

"Did you listen to anything I said last night?"

Yes. All of it.

"You will be ill. You are ill."

"I am not ill."

"You will be ill, if you don't stay in today. You need to rest."

"I don't need to rest. I can't rest."

"Besides," says Gran, "you haven't had breakfast."

I don't take on the breakfast issue. I just say, "No one stays in when it snows, Gran. Everyone goes out. They play."

"You played last night," says Gran grimly. And then she takes the large brass key that fits the bottom lock on our front door, the anti-burglar Chubb lock, and slots

231

it in. She turns her wrist with something like triumph.

She is locking me in.

She is locking me in my own house.

"You can't do that," I say.

"Can't I?" she replies, and she drops the key in the pocket of her apron.

There's only one thing for it, I'll have to make a run for it. I haven't time for a jacket, I haven't time for wellington boots, or a scarf, or a hat, or gloves. I just run, in my socks, down the hall and through the kitchen and unbolt and unlock the back door (which does not have a Chubb fitting) and I tear out into the garden (where I nearly stop immediately as my feet land in the freezing wet snow), and around the side of the house and into the street.

"No," shouts Gran.

But she isn't even close to being behind me.

55

Running isn't exactly an option, what with the thick wet of the snow and the surprisingly hard and uneven pavement below, but I'm still moving fast. As fast as I can. At the bottom of the cul-de-sac I pass the ice mermaid. Her proud, beautiful head and carved ice eyes watch me pass. She is intact, so the snow babies will be too.

I'm glad of my jeans and my shirt and thick fleece hoodie, but my feet are already in pain and so are my hands. The wind is managing to find the gap around my throat and send icy blasts down the front of my chest, but I just stumble on, not caring. At least the speed is helping, the stumble-running is warming my core, that space around my heart.

I pass the electricity junction box at the edge of the

park. It's still humming, though you can hardly hear it for the shouts and yells and laughter coming from the park. The park is full of brightly coloured people shrieking as they toboggan down slopes on sledges and tin trays and flattened cardboard boxes. There are mothers and fathers and tiny children all muffled up and dogs barking. One little grey dog has a series of tiny snowballs attached to all four paws which he's trying, in vain, to bite off. I think I recognise some people from school at the top of the hill by the conker tree, though everyone is twice their normal size in ski jackets and snow boots. Closer to me, in the play park, a child is eating snow from a swing and being reprimanded.

It's all so very ordinary.

Most people are busy with what they are doing, but some turn as I pass and one child even points, maybe because I'm stumble-running still, maybe because I don't look dressed for the snow.

I'm soon at the bowling green. I can no longer feel my feet. I think they have joined some other body. Or maybe they've become part of the frozen earth; they certainly don't seem to be mine any more. My head takes no responsibility for them. Or for my hands.

The gate of the bowling green is wide open. *No Dogs.*
No Ball Games.

It doesn't say anything about the Pavement Crack
Game.

There are four dogs in the area and a huge snowball
fight in progress, right at the centre of which is beach-
ball-grinning Paddy. Sam is with him, and Alice. And
also Em. Em is back.

Do I care?

No. I don't care about Em or Alice. I don't even
care about Zoe who now I see is crouching, face to
the ground, gathering snow. Whether Zoe's smiling,
whether she's read the letter – it all seems totally
unimportant. The only thing that matters now is the
babies. Protecting them.

You can't see the bench from the gate, so I know
nothing until I turn in and pass the shivering palm tree.

There they are, snow Richie, snow Clem, just as I
left them.

No, not just as I left them, they are slightly more
slumped, slightly closer together, their little heads have
gone crystalline.

I will sit with them all day if I have to.

All night. All day again. As long as it takes.

"Jess, is that you? Jess. Jess!" Em is coming over. "Yay – Jess!"

"Hey, what's with the footwear, Jess?" Paddy is coming too.

"Bombs away," shouts Zoe. Now she's looking up, standing up, and she is smiling, widely, broadly. Grinning like a lunatic. She lobs a snowball at Paddy, which catches him right on the side of his head.

"Oi!" he yells. He's less than an arm's length away from me, and to retaliate, I think he's just going to bend down and scoop snow from beneath his feet. But he doesn't. He's in a rush so he just leans forwards and grabs Clem's already neatly balled head.

"No!" I scream.

But he's already done it. He's taken Clem's head and he's lobbing it at Zoe. It flies through the air, but his aim is wide and he misses her.

Zoe does her tribal victory dance. She's stamping and yelling and whistling and GRINNING.

"No! No! NO!" I cry.

"What's up with you?" says Paddy.

I could hit him, push him, kill him, put the whole force of my body between him and what remains of the babies. But I do nothing. I just stand there completely unable to move, staring at headless Clem and also the join. The join — the babies are still joined. Maybe that's enough, could that be enough? It's my game, my Pavement Crack Game, it wouldn't be changing the rules to say, it's the join that matters, if the join survives, then…

"Bombs away," shouts Zoe again. And it's coming at me this time, a huge white ball of snow flying through the air alongside Zoe's ecstatic GRIN. I observe myself stepping aside; I do it instinctively, so as not to be hit.

So the biggest snowball in the world makes a perfect parabola over the bowling green and lands smack between the babies, right on the join.

Splitting them asunder.

56

I don't know why or how I move after that. There is no part of my body I can feel, my bones are solid ice, yet I'm moving.

I brought it on myself, didn't I? The death of Clem, of Zoe and me, of everything I've ever wanted. If I was looking for a message — what could be clearer? Headless Clem. Smashed-up join. If I believe in pictures and symbols and things without words, what more is there to say?

"Jess?" Someone is behind me. It isn't Em or Alice or Paddy. They're all still screeching in the park. "Jess. Jess!" It's Zoe. Screeching Zoe.

Her voice just one of many because no one's laughing any more. All the mothers and all the fathers and all the children are screeching, they're screaming, wailing, crying, their noise like fingers down a blackboard in my ears, because there can never be any happiness.

Not now.

Not ever.

"Jess!"

"Leave me alone."

But she doesn't.

Haven't we played this scene before? Jessica Walton fleeing the park pursued by her friend Zoe? And it doesn't end well, it ends with Jess screaming: *I'll never tell you anything ever again.* Only this time Zoe's still coming.

"It's over. It's all over. Can you see that? I've lost, you've lost, the babies have lost—"

"Lost what?"

"Everything."

The snow mermaid is still outside Bruno Teisler's garage. It remains proud, beautiful and intact. I punch that mermaid's head off.

"Jess?" It's difficult to hear Zoe's voice above the screeching, but I do hear it. It's full of horror. And fear. "What's got into you?"

"Go away, Zoe. Forget it. Forget everything I wrote in that letter. It's over. Finished."

Zoe does not go away. "What letter?" she says.

"The one I wrote last night, posted through your front door last night."

"So what if I came out my back door this morning?"

"Did you come out your back door?"

"Why are we even having this conversation? Jess…"

"Just Go Away!"

But she's still right by me when I arrive at my own back door. I expect to see the towering figure of Gran, but there is no Gran. Gran must be wandering the park, the streets. Gran must be saying to every passing stranger: *Have you seen my granddaughter? She's lost. Lost. You must have seen her, she went out without shoes, without boots. Have you seen her? Have you seen her lying in the snow?*

I go into the house and Zoe follows.

"Jess, please, tell me, just tell me."

Zoe is back in my house.

"Whatever it is," Zoe says, "we can work it out."

We.

We can work it out.

"Look, OK, I know I haven't exactly been, well, oh, Jess… you know what? You scare me. You're so wrapped up in yourself right now. I can't get access to you any more. I don't know who you are any more, Jess. Are you hearing me, Jess?"

I'm hearing her and the other noises, the screeching ones, they're getting a little quieter. She's come. She didn't get the letter and she's come. Anyway.

I stop running.

She puts out her hand, touches me on the shoulder.

"Jeez," she says, "you are so cold."

She slips off her wellies and her jacket and pushes me through to the kitchen.

"How can anyone be that cold?"

I stand there and suddenly, like Roger the Wreck, I just rattle. My teeth rattle, my bones rattle, my mind rattles and shivers go up and down my body in continuous waves.

"You've got to get warm," Zoe says, and she tries to hold my hands in hers, but even the faint difference in temperature (Zoe's hands are not warm, but they're warmer than mine) makes me cry out with pain.

"Get those clothes off," says Zoe. "Get those stupid socks off."

But I can't bend and my fingers won't work.

She makes me lie down, right there on the kitchen floor, and she pulls at all the wet clothes and still I shiver.

"Rug," she says. "You need a rug. Where's a rug? No, bed. You'd be better off in bed. Or a bath. Yes, that's it. You should go in the bath."

I don't resist, I just let her push me up the stairs and I sit on the bathroom stool while she runs the water. I notice I still have my underwear on, but that seems wet through too.

"Take it off," she says, nodding at my vest and pants, and when I just continue to sit there, she comes to help me.

And then I'm naked.

Which is OK.

With Zoe.

"Get in."

I try my toe in the water and shriek with pain.

"What is it?"

"Too hot."

She puts her hand in the water, stirs it about. "It's not that hot. It's fine." But she puts some more cold in anyway. "Maybe your body…" She doesn't finish the sentence.

And then I get in. Then I lie in the warmish water and let my body thaw.

Tears well out of my eyes.

"Don't cry," says Zoe. "Why are you crying?"

And I don't know if it's the warmth of the water or

the warmth of we, or whether it's just my body giving up, giving in.

"I don't know," I say.

She sloshes some water over my belly. "It's not about Easter, is it?" she says. "Or Paddy. It's not about any of that stupid stuff, is it?"

I look right into her mirror eyes.

"Did you like going to the film with him?"

"With who?"

"Paddy."

"When did I go to a film with Paddy?"

"Yesterday. When you couldn't come with me – to the Buddhist Centre."

"Who said I went with Paddy? I went with my cousin – Savvy. I went with the family."

The water is lap lap lapping around my body. Or slap slap slapping. Stupid, stupid, stupid Jess. Jumping to Conclusions – that's what Si calls it. Sensible people, says Si, do not jump to conclusions.

"Though I don't see why I shouldn't go with Paddy. Not if I want to."

"No. You're right," I say. "You're right, Zoe. I mean a person can love two people at the same time, right? Like just because I love Clem, doesn't mean I've nothing left over for Richie, does it?"

"Huh?" Zoe stares at me. "I'm not sure where love comes into this. Not with me and Paddy, anyway. I mean, he's a laugh, he's fun to have around but… well, if I wanted to go to see a film, I'd probably rather go with you."

"With me?"

"Yes, with you, stupid."

Water slaps about me.

"And just for the record," continues Zoe, "I didn't tell Paddy about the babies being joined either. Alice did that."

The water slaps some more. "Alice?" Stupid Jess repeats.

"Yes, Alice. You told Em and Em told Alice."

How to Be Your Own Worst Enemy. Zoe is right, I've been so wrapped up inside my own head I've forgotten that other people exist, that they have lives and thoughts all of their own. I've blamed Zoe and hated her and all along it was just me. Jumping to conclusions. Making stuff up. They've always said that about me. I just make stuff up.

I think I'm sobbing now. "I'm so sorry, Zoe."

"Well, don't be. And stop that crying too. You have

244

to stop, Jess. And you have to tell me what this is really all about. Please."

She hands me some toilet tissue on which to blow my nose. And after I've done that, I tell her.

I tell Zoe everything.

57

It pours out of me like I'm some waterfall that just fell over a beautiful rock. I'm rushing and rushing to tell Zoe about the colour of the skin where the babies join and how I felt when I saw it that first ever time, and about the operation being brought forward and the light in the flask guttering and about the snow babies and the pavement crack monsters, and how that, if the snow babies ceased to exist before the op, then both boys would die.

Will die.

Temporarily, I keep back the bit about how I also chucked our friendship over my shoulder like salt, for good luck.

Zoe doesn't laugh once, not once.

"Then that's all right then," she says.

"What?"

"If it's about still existing – did you say *still exist* or *not melt* or *not be destroyed*?"

And I look at her hard, to see if she's just humouring me. But no, there's something intense and piercing in her eyes, as if she really wants to be in the same mad space as me, because she knows how important it is to me.

"I don't understand," I say. "What are you getting at?"

"Just tell me," Zoe orders. She fumbles in her pocket and brings out her phone. "*Exist* or *not melt*?"

"I said they had to exist," I say.

"Well, they do," says Zoe. She flicks her phone to camera. "Look."

I lean out of the bath. The heat is making the screen hazy. "Look," Zoe repeats, flicking through some pictures. There's a winter wonderland panorama of the whole park, a picture of a pink scarf tied around a bollard, a shot of Paddy sledging with Sam on a tray, a close-up of a giant snowball ("Alice and I made that," she says), and then, finally, there are the snow babies on their bench, their little heads nestling against each other.

"I don't believe it," I say.

247

"Believe it," says Zoe. "They exist. I captured them." She pauses. "And do you want to know why I took the picture? Because when I first saw them, they reminded me of me and you. You know, when we were about four or five and we used to…"

"… snuggle up on a sofa together," I say.

"Yes, and watch…"

"*The Snowman*," we say together.

I want the moment to last for ever, but there's something else I have a pounding need to know. I start scrambling out of the bath.

"Where are you going?"

I grab for a towel, trail along the corridor and Zoe trails after me.

"Where are you going now?"

In my room, on my bedside table, is the flask.

I'm stumble-running all over again, stretching out my warm – trembling – hands. I clutch the flask close, and look and look. Through the transparent whorls of glass the colours shine. The threads of yellowy gold, deeper now, more intense, intertwined, curled together into some light, bright mist. And there's a seed fish swimming. No. No! Two seed fish swimming – there they are, sparking the air.

"Two!" I shout. "Look, Zoe, two!"

"Two? Two what?"

"So you're right, you must be right. You've done it. They're going to live. They're going to be all right. The babies. Both of them. Oh, thank you, thank you, thank you, Zoe. Thank you for ever!"

I fling my arms around her, feel my head rest a moment on her shoulder, my chest lie flush with hers, and because I am smaller than her and all curled up, my heart beat against hers.

"Thank me," says Zoe, "or that bottle?"

Which is when I realise that there's something I've left out.

"It's a flask," I say, and I pull away a little.

"Yes," says Zoe, "I remember. *Big as a storm wind, tiny as a baby's breath.* Right?"

"Yes."

She raises an eyebrow, but I've started now and I have to go on and I want to go on. I want to share with Zoe the most difficult thing of all.

"This bottle, this flask…" I begin.

"Yes?"

"It isn't empty." I'm still afraid; I'm afraid of saying it out loud. "It contains something."

249

"What?"

"Well, I don't really know. I know it has something to do with Clem, because when Clem's not well the flask howls." I tell her about the pulsing blackness. "Or it goes very dim and defeated. Gutters." I tell her about the flattened flame. "But that could be to do with me, because sometimes, I think, if I'm bad, the flask suffers."

"Suffers?"

"Yes."

"But you're never bad," says Zoe simply. "You haven't got a bad bone in your body."

"Huh?" That would be something to think about, but I don't have time because I need to get to Rob. "It's also got to do with this person – Rob. In fact, the flask can sing, a song called 'For Rob', which is really beautiful, but sad at the same time. It makes you want to cry, hard as rain, beautiful as a rainbow."

"You're really losing me now," says Zoe.

I can see how ridiculous it all sounds. Especially Rob and his song. Rob who I still don't know anything about except that he's to do with Aunt Edie. And I haven't even got to the fizz-heart blue and the strips of paper moonlight yet.

"I'm not explaining this very well," I say.

But Zoe is, for once, all patience and I know how difficult it must be for her so I try harder.

"You remember," I say, "when we were at the Buddhist Centre and Lalitavajri talked about consciousnesses and how they have to wait around and… well, sometimes I think that the thing in this flask is, um, like that." I finish lamely.

"What?" says Zoe. "You mean – a soul?"

And so it's her who finally says it, lays it like a jewel between us.

"Yes," I say, relieved. "A soul. One that maybe hasn't found its place yet."

"You mean it missed its sex slot?"

Trust Zoe to mention that. "Sort of. Or one that just got left behind. Lost."

"A lost soul," says Zoe, and she's still not laughing.

There's a silence.

If I'm mad, she's mad too now.

"Zoe," I say, "will you tell me something truthfully?"

"Of course."

I put the flask in her hands. "Tell me what you see."

Zoe turns the flask over. And over. Just like I did the first time I ever held it.

"Well," she says carefully, "I see a bottle, a flask,

which is very beautiful really, with little silvery lines and whorls and stuff in the glass that looks like little seeds."

"Or fish," I say.

"Yes, or fish."

"And are they swimming? Are two of those seed fish swimming?"

"Swimming?" says Zoe. "No, I don't think so."

"What about inside?"

"Inside," says Zoe, "it's sort of misty, but bright as well."

"And is that misty-bright something ordinary – or not?"

"Well," she says again, "I think it's just the light, the way the light plays through the glass."

"You don't see colours?"

Zoe looks up at me. "What colours?"

"Yellow? Gold?"

"No, not really." Zoe pauses. "But you do, don't you?"

"Yes."

"Same as you heard the howls and Rob's song."

"Yes."

Another silence.

"Am I mad, Zoe?"

Zoe puts the flask down very carefully, and then she turns to me and puts her hands on my shoulders. "I think you're extraordinary," she says.

"That's not the answer to the question."

"I think it is. I think maybe some people have, I don't know, thinner skins than other people. Feel things differently. I think you're one of those people. Like you and music. You feel it differently from everyone else."

"No I don't," I protest. "You feel just the same about dance."

"No, I don't actually," says Zoe. "I dance to other people's tunes. You – you sing stuff that comes right from deep inside you."

"Does that mean I can spot a soul when I see one?"

"Not necessarily. But you are open to possibilities. I don't know about this Rob, or how the flask tells you when stuff is wrong with Clem, I don't know anything about that. But I believe you."

She believes me.

"And I think you should believe yourself. Trust your instinct. That's all. I can't really say any more."

But she has said enough.

I hug her tighter than I ever did over the Cadbury's

creme egg. This time, she hugs me back. So there we are in my bedroom – totally separate, yet joined.

58

We are so involved in our conversation that we do not hear the front door latch and we are embracing when there are treads on the stairs. So we hear nothing until the door opens, and standing in the door frame, still in her outside coat, is Gran. She is not towering, she is not angry, in fact, she just looks old and frail and exhausted.

"I'm sorry," I say immediately. "I'm really sorry, Gran."

And she doesn't shout. Not at all. She just presses her lips tight together, as if she's trying to hold in some emotion, and her eyes squeeze up, and despite the outdoor coat, a big shudder goes through the whole of her body.

And then I go over to her, one hand holding the towel around me, one hand around her neck.

And she kisses the top of my head.

Kisses me.

There's a long moment of silence and I feel (but cannot see) her looking out over my head and finally noticing Zoe.

"Hello Mrs Walton," says Zoe.

"Hello Zoe," says Gran.

"Zoe helped me," I say. "It was Zoe who got me home, got me warm."

Gran looks at Zoe and then at me and she nods. "Thank you, Zoe," says Gran. "Thank you very much." Then she adds, "Why don't you put on a dressing gown, Jess, while I make us some tea and toast. Would you like toast, Zoe?"

And it's the dressing gown that takes me by surprise. Gran is not a dressing gown person. More particularly, she is not in favour of people eating breakfast in their dressing gowns. She calls it *slack*. Gran thinks people who are going to make something of their lives get dressed in the morning.

Gran escorts Zoe out of the room and I slip on my nightie, dressing gown and slippers. In the pocket of the dressing gown, I put the flask.

Then I go downstairs and we all sit around the

kitchen table and the mugs of tea steam and I eat four slices of hot buttered toast.

Eventually Zoe says thank you and she needs to be getting home, else her mum will worry (at this Gran flashes a not-quite-so-benign look at me) and then she turns to me.

"Bye Jess," she says.

"Bye," I say, "my best friend in the whole universe."

Zoe smiles.

When she's gone, I expect Gran to turn around and ask me to explain myself. But she doesn't. More than this, she allows me to be in my dressing gown all day and all evening.

I think I love my gran.

59

The next day it's as if the snow never existed. I look out of the window and I am astonished. The whole world has turned green and the sun is out. The sun is shining brilliantly.

I come downstairs (dressed) to see Gran staring out of the kitchen window.

"It's an omen," she says.

And I nod, because neither of us has to say the word *operation*, it just hangs in the air of the house. I imagine the babies being wheeled down the long corridor towards the operating theatre, Mum and Si walking close behind, holding hands, joined. I see the anaesthetists checking charts and flicking syringes and Mum and Si just looking at the babies' faces as though it could be for the last time.

Which is what you would feel if you didn't know

how brightly the flask is shining this morning.

"How can it all have just gone?" I ask Gran of the snowless world.

"I've only seen it once before like this," says Gran. "When I was a little girl, about the same age as you. Only that time it was just one day. It snowed in the night, really heavy snow, and in the morning we went out sledging with a sled my father made himself, and then, by the afternoon of the same day, there was nothing left at all. It was like a dream."

Gran opens the back door. "Feel it," she says. "Feel how warm it is."

And I go and stand outside and feel the sun on my face and that reminds me of the mesembryanthemums in Aunt Edie's garden and how their faces opened to the sun, and I feel something open out in me too.

"Shall we go out?" I say to Gran. "Before breakfast?"

There is no *before breakfast* in Gran's life. Nothing can be achieved before breakfast.

"Yes," says Gran. "Let's."

We put on jackets, but we could almost have gone out in T-shirts, short sleeves anyway. We walk down the close and take great gulps of air.

"It smells of…" I begin.

"… of summer," Gran finishes.

"What is that smell?"

"I don't know," says Gran, sniffing again. "I'd like to say it's flowers. But it isn't. It's just… a kind of warmth."

"A promise," I say.

"A promise?"

"That summer will come. That after the winter, summer will come."

In my pocket, the flask that was so cold is warm to the touch.

"I'm not sure you can smell a promise," says Gran.

But I think you can.

We pass the garage where Bruno Teisler built the ice mermaid. Not a single crystal of snow remains. Which is strange too, because isn't it the compacted snow that usually remains? The giant snowballs, the thick trunks of snowmen? They sit solid for days no matter how green the grass around them. The lack of any trace of the mermaid makes me feel slightly (but only slightly) better about knocking her head off.

We're not aiming for the park, we haven't discussed where we're going, but Gran and I arrive at the park.

Some blossom trees are out, not the heavy pink cherry kind, but the lighter paler sort.

"Apple," says Gran. "It's apple."

And I look through the blossom up into the sky, which is a very pale blue with high, wispy clouds.

But it's not sky or the blossom that's so extraordinary, it's the tiny shoots of green on almost every tree and bush and plant in the park. They look to me suddenly like tiny green flames, as if the whole park will soon combust in a great conflagration of green.

"Look at the flower buds," says Gran.

And I hadn't noticed those.

Tight buds on the rose bushes, their delicate pinks masked with a kind of papery, brown exterior petal.

"And this is choisya, I think," says Gran, bending down to examine a dark green bush dense with tiny white buds. "It will smell amazing in a few weeks."

The whole park is pulsing with the promise of new life.

Then we see the butterfly.

"It's a Red Admiral," I say, "isn't it?"

Gran nods and I concentrate on its bright colours and its delicate, delicate, beating wings.

"How could it survive?" I ask Gran. "How could it survive the snow?"

"I don't know," she says. "Maybe it didn't. Maybe it

came out of its chrysalis just this morning."

I don't know if this is true, but I want it to be true. I want this beautiful creature to have been born today, liberated today, come into the world today. This day of my brothers' operation.

Beating wing.

Beating heart.

I watch it flutter from bush to bush, looking for some place of welcome, an open flower, then flutter on, searching wider, trying harder. And then just lift into the sky where I watch it, outlined against the sky.

Then I have the strangest sense that I too am fluttering, growing, promising. That I'm totally myself, Jessica Walton, but that I'm also a leaf unfurling, a rosebud waiting to bloom, a cloud scudding across the sky, a butterfly on the wing. That I belong to myself, but also to the whole world, that I'm part of it, every cell of mine indivisible from every other cell in the universe. It only lasts a moment this feeling, but it pierces me with happiness and with hope.

"Gran?" I say.

"Yes, Jess?"

"Can we go to Aunt Edie's house?"

"Why?" asks Gran.

"I want to play the piano."

60

She takes me to Aunt Edie's in the afternoon.

"Might as well," she says. The sun is still shining, but Gran's mood has darkened. She's thinking, but not saying, that this is about the most dangerous time for the twins, Phase 4, when the team of surgeons will divide their single liver.

"We can't discount the possibility of haemorrhage." That's what the doctors say. That's what they fear. In her dark afternoon, Gran is afraid.

I am not afraid.

The flask is green.

Not lurid, electric green as it was when it stood in front of the green buttons of my Wi-Fi router, but the bold, gorgeous green of nature. It came in, a flame at a time, with the tiny shoots of new life on the trees in the park. It pushed itself through the misty white and gold, like young blades of grass. All through the day the green has come, promising pulsing spring. Now there is nothing left of white and gold, the flask is just one whole globe of green.

We don't go through the little side gate; we park in Gran's drive and walk around the road way to Aunt Edie's front door.

"I've got the piano men coming next week," Gran says. "This will be the last time you can play the piano in Edie's house."

And previously that would have chilled me, but it doesn't today because today is full of hope and glory.

I go straight to Aunt Edie's sitting room and I hope Gran won't follow me and she doesn't. Perhaps she knows I need to be alone now.

I set the shining green world of the flask on top of the piano.

"Now," I say. "It's now, isn't it?"

I can hear the notes, of course I can, they began to come when we walked in the park. They pushed into my mind along with the blades of grass.

I lay my hand on the hair from the lion's mane, and around it a chord builds, quite easily, fluently, as though it could never be or have been any chord but the one that finds itself under my fingers. It makes me think of Aunt Edie and how music flowed out of her hands. Alongside the lion are other notes from 'For Rob', but they don't make you want to cry, they are not a lament. It's the same music, but not the same music at all, it's a mirror reflection, stronger, more powerful. I realise then where this song is heading, what the mirror is: all the minor chords of 'For Rob', they have parallels in the major keys. If I can stretch my hands and my mind then I will find this jubilant thing, this thing that has been just out of my reach for so long.

"It's what you showed me in the park?" I say to the flask. "Yes?"

This possibility, this song which says that God's creation cannot fail. Everything counts: the tiniest trill of the sweetest bird to the loudest most crashing crescendo wave. They all have their part to play in the whole beautiful pattern and rhythm of life. Only I still can't hear it all, there's something missing.

"What is it? Tell me! You must know this song. You sang it first."

The flask glows and glows.

But the ending will not come. It makes me feel like

I'm on the edge of a cliff suspended – I could fall, I could fly, fall, fly…

The door opens.

Someone comes in.

It's not Gran.

It's no one I know. In fact, it's three people I don't know.

Three people in Aunt Edie's house, I haven't heard coming because I've been all wrapped up in the music.

I fall. Or at least my hands do – off the piano.

There's a man in a sharp suit with a fat tie and scrubbed-clean face who looks startled, and a young couple, at least I think they're a couple, because of the way they're standing, so close they're almost joined, barely a kiss apart.

"That was nice," says the woman, nodding at the piano. "Really nice."

Nice. This song of creation.

Nice.

But she means it kindly, I see that. She's got warm brown eyes.

The fat tie man taps at his clipboard. "I wasn't expecting anyone," he says, "to be in."

Then I see what the woman is carrying. A sheet of

paper with a picture of Aunt Edie's house on it, and below the picture, details of all Aunt Edie's rooms, the precise measurements, a layout of the ground floor, a layout of the first floor. And a price.

Aunt Edie's house is for sale and here is the estate agent and a couple who might come into this house and repaint the walls (well, actually they need repainting), and fill the rooms with their own furniture, and perhaps have a baby here. A baby of their own.

"You're her granddaughter," says Fat Tie. "Is that right? Mrs Walton's granddaughter?"

I say nothing.

"Nice room," says the man, beginning to explore, to look out of Aunt Edie's bay window. "Spacious."

The woman hasn't moved though. "Don't let us disturb you," she says again. "You just go right on playing."

But, of course, I can't.

The husband comes up behind his wife and slides his hand around her waist. "Your piano would fit here," he says. "Wouldn't it?"

"Yes," she says.

And then Fat Tie says, "Of course, the conservatory is a huge asset to the house," and he takes them through the Sun Room and out into the garden.

I want to start the song again, but I can't. There is only one way back into the house and it's through this room. Even if Fat Tie takes the couple right to the end of the witch's hat garden where the compost heap is, and even if they stop off on the way back to inspect the gate through to Gran's garden or observe how her eucalyptus tree leans over the joint fence, they will not be gone very long. They will be back, disturbing my song again.

I pick the flask up off the piano, hold it in my hands. It's green and quiet.

"But you don't mind, do you?"

No reply.

"You could have sung and you didn't. Yes?"

No reply.

"So when? If not now? When?"

No reply.

I put the flask back on the piano. I will have to wait again. Listen. Be patient.

"A song always chooses its own time. Yes?"

I can hear voices from the garden. I haven't thought of the people coming to buy Aunt Edie's house before. I've blocked them out, not wanting anyone to tread in the sacred places that were Edie's. Edie's and mine.

But if someone has to buy this house, I hope suddenly that it will be this young couple with their near-kiss join and their hopes and their piano. Or her piano anyway.

Soon enough they're back.

Fat Tie is all for pushing them quickly through the room, but the woman hovers, comes close to the piano, looks at me, looks at the flask.

"That's a very beautiful object," she says. "I like the way," she pauses, "it seems to capture the light."

"Capture the light?" I repeat.

Can she see it? Can this total stranger see it?

"Yes," she says. "It's very unusual, isn't it?" She smiles. "Like your playing," she adds. "Did you make up that piece yourself?"

"Sort of," I say.

She nods. "If we buy this house," she says, "I will always remember you. You – and your music."

Then I'm pierced again with a hope and a happiness, which lasts right up until the evening.

When Si rings.

61

Although we have been waiting for the call all day, we still both jump when the phone rings. Gran nods at me to pick up, as if some part of her cannot bear to know what we have waited so long to know.

"Jess?" Si is bleary with exhaustion. "They're back on the ward, Jess."

They're back on the ward.

They are.

They.

"They're back on the ward," I shout at Gran. "Both of them are back on the ward! Told you. Told you, told you, told you!"

Gran lifts her hand to her chest, crosses herself.

Si is silent. Si is not joining in the jubilation.

"What?" I say.

"Richie's good. Richie's doing really well." He pauses.

"And Clem?"

"The next twenty-four hours," says Si, "they're going to be critical for Clem."

"But he's going to be fine," I say. In my pocket is the flask. It's still a brilliant, gorgeous green. I've checked every five minutes since we returned from Gran's. I check again. "He's going to be fine."

"I wish I had your confidence," says Si quietly. "Now, can I talk to Gran?"

I hand over the phone and Gran listens and listens and says nothing. After what seems like a lifetime she finally speaks. "Tomorrow then," she says. "We'll come early. We'll be there as soon as we can."

62

"What?" I say to Gran. "What?"

"Clem," she says.

"I know Clem," I exclaim. "But what?"

"The operation went really well, better than they expected. No hitches at all."

"So?"

"So they can't explain it. Why Clem isn't doing better than he is."

I can't explain it either. The snow babies exist. The flask is green, both seed fishes are swimming. Both of them.

I ring Zoe. "Can you come round?"

"It's late," she says. "Really late."

"I know."

Zoe comes around.

"This is a bit late," says Gran.

"It's important," Zoe and I say together, not a breath between our words.

"It may be…" begins Gran. "But people have to sleep."

"I'm not sure I'll be sleeping tonight," I say. "Will you?"

Gran lets Zoe in.

We go to my room. I put the flask on the bureau.

"What do you see?" I ask.

"Not much, I'm afraid," she says.

"But does it look the same, the same as it did before?"

"Brighter possibly. With a tinge of something."

"Tinge of what?"

"Colour?"

"Green," I say. "It's green." I tell her about my day, about the park and the green and the song and how everything has to be OK, only it isn't.

"He's critical," I tell Zoe.

"Have they said that?"

"Yes. Good as."

Zoe picks up the flask.

"Pity it can't talk," she says. "Then it could tell us what to do." As she turns the flask about in her hands, her fingers seem to tremble, or else she's just clumsy,

273

and the flask falls, it falls out of her grip.

"No!" I cry.

But of course, the flask doesn't fall far, it's only an inch or so to the desk, so it simply skids a little, knocks into one of the wooden pillars that stand either side of the arch that houses ScatCat and the friendship bracelets.

The pillar wobbles.

"Oh – I'm so sorry," Zoe says, grasping the perfectly strong flask and righting it again.

"Did you see that?" I ask.

"Of course I did, it was me who dropped it," she says.

"No," I say. "The pillar."

"What?"

I stretch out my hand, and touch it. It moves again.

"Loose bit of wood?" says Zoe.

But I know it isn't and actually she knows it isn't either. At least it is a loose bit of wood, but it wobbles not as if it's broken, but sturdily, as if there's a purpose to its wobbling. My heart gives a little thump, just as it did when I discovered the too-short drawer which hid the flask. I put my hand up to the curved wooden surface of the column and I pull. I expect it to give way immediately, but it doesn't.

"Let me try," Zoe says. She jigs with her fingers, pushes her nails, which are longer than mine and painted a vivid red, into the gap between the pillar and the surrounding surfaces. And there's the answer: it's not just the pillar that's loose, but the apparently solid piece of mounting behind.

"You do it," she says suddenly.

Is she afraid? Beautiful, bold Zoe?

My smaller, quieter hands get to work. I readjust my grip and pull. This time, pillar and mounting come straight out, revealing themselves as the front end of a small, perfectly crafted compartment about one inch wide and eight inches deep. The sort of place you might hide a document or a letter. Thrum, thrum, thrum goes my heart. And from the look on Zoe's face, so does hers.

But the slim wooden box is empty. I turn it upside down and tap it on the bottom, just to make sure. There's nothing in it at all, not even an old button or a pin.

"Oh," says Zoe, somewhere between disappointed and relieved.

I'm already turning my attention to the second pillar. Of the bureau's two 'matching' drawers only one actually concealed a secret space, so it I shouldn't expect the second pillar to move...

But it does.

It wobbles just like its twin.

Its twin.

A little pair of pillars. Joined.

"Oh, oh," says Zoe again.

I pull out the second pillar. It conceals an identical one inch by eight inch secret space. Only this box isn't empty.

"What is it?" says Zoe.

"Don't know."

Thrum. Thrum. Thrum.

It contains an envelope.

I shake it out on to the desk and it lands upside down, so I have to turn it over to read the writing.

For Rob, it says.

Am I surprised? No, I am not surprised. Nothing surprises me any more. Especially when it's part of a pattern. You think things end, but they don't, they begin all over again. Like summer follows winter or night follows day.

"Don't open it," says Zoe.

"I have to." The loopy black writing is Aunt Edie's. "It's from my aunt."

"From her, but not to you," remarks Zoe.

"It's not stuck down." And it isn't. It's one of those old-fashioned envelopes you have to lick. "If Aunt Edie didn't want anyone looking in this envelope she could have licked it up. But she didn't."

"Even so," says Zoe.

"Look," I say. "It was you who said 'pity you can't talk'. Well, maybe the flask just did."

"OK," says Zoe. "Do it."

She's talking like the envelope is an unexploded bomb. And it is, in a way, or so I find when I tip its contents out.

There's just one sheet of pale cream paper without an address.

My darling, darling boy, it begins.

"Read it out," says Zoe.

So I do.

My darling, darling boy

You will never read this — one of a lifetime of things you'll never do — so I don't really know why I'm writing it. Except I have to talk to someone and the only one I want to talk to right now is you.

It's just four hours since they took you out of my arms. They didn't want me to hold you at all, they said it would be 'easier' that way. Easier not to hold my own son?

You just looked asleep, a baby snuggled in some blankets having a nap. You fooled me with your beautiful face and your perfect little lips. You'd wake at any moment, I thought, wake and open your eyes and look at me.

That's why I couldn't leave you alone in the cot, even when I had to go to the bathroom. I couldn't bear the thought of you waking alone, waking when I wasn't there.

When they came to take you away I didn't cry. I didn't scream, not out loud anyway. I just thought, as the little white shawl of you disappeared through the door: I should have unwrapped you. Why didn't I unwrap you? I never saw you naked, never held you skin to skin. Never saw your feet.

And now I'm back home, sitting at my ordinary desk, writing with my ordinary pen. Writing to you. But perhaps you already know that? Because now I'm not so sure you've gone after all. I can still feel you, really close. I can feel the breath you never took on my cheek. So do you know what I think, darling boy? I think one day you'll wake after all. And when that day comes, I'm going to be right beside you still.

Until then, my darling boy, keep safe.

Love you for ever.

I pause. I can barely say the last word.

"What?" says Zoe.

"Mummy," I read.

63

I'm wrong about not being surprised any more. My head is zinging with surprise. I see (as if she was in the room) Aunt Edie holding her dead child in her arms. Because that's what it means, doesn't it? That Aunt Edie had a son, Rob, a baby born dead.

"That's so sad," Zoe says, all ghostly quiet.

"Yes," I say, zinging. "And no."

"No?"

"Well, yes – of course *yes*." The very idea of Aunt Edie holding her dead child is enough to tear my heart out. "Sad then – but not now." I pause. "Don't you see?"

"What? See what?"

I hold up the shimmering green flask. "This. What this could actually be?"

"A soul, you said a soul… oh, my gosh," Zoe says.

"I *can still feel you really close*. That's what she said. All those years ago."

"No."

"Yes," I say. "It has to be."

"But what's that… that thing got to do with Clem?"

"Everything. Remember when I was out in the park, when I put the flask between the snow babies? You remember? And it sort of slipped, or Clem took it, under his arm. And it looked like the flask *belonged* somehow, and I thought that Clem was saying something, or the flask was saying something…"

"What? Saying what?"

"Zoe – if you were a soul, a lost soul, the soul of a little boy who died, what would you want?"

"A body." Zoe's whispering. "I'd want a body."

"Yes. Of course. Which is why it must have kept coming back to the bottle, to a thing that looks a little like a ribcage, to the only place of safety it could probably find. But inside this hard hard glass, you'd never give up looking, would you?" I think of all the times the breath sat on the window sill looking out. "You'd be wanting, yearning… searching for your real other half, your perfect match…"

"… your twin," says Zoe.

"Yes." We hold each other's gaze a moment. "And Clem," I go on. "Think about Clem." My mind is rushing again. "Why do you think nothing's making any difference? The doctors, the medicine? It all went so well. That's what Gran said. So the doctors can't understand why Clem isn't doing better than he is."

"Because he has something missing too."

"Yes. It has to be. Richie always had more of everything. He was – he is – the bigger twin. He didn't have the damaged heart. He had a greater share of the liver…"

"And now they're separated," Zoe says, "you think Richie's got the greater share of their joint soul?"

"Yes. Or all of it maybe. What if Richie has all that life force pounding in him and little Clem has nothing?"

"Which is why he's fading…"

"Yes. Exactly. Because it's not just a body that makes us alive, is it? Whatever Pug says about Mrs Nerg. We're not just blood and bones." I hold up the shining flask. "We're something more."

I come to a breathless pause.

"You have to get to the hospital," says Zoe. "You have to go right now."

I run into the corridor where Gran is making preparations for bed.

"We have to go to the hospital," I shout at her. "We have to go now."

"Don't be ridiculous," says Gran. "It's nearly eleven o'clock."

"No, you don't understand. We have to go now."

"We're going tomorrow, first thing. That's time enough."

"It isn't, he won't last that long."

"I don't know what you're talking about."

I hold up the flask. I'm talking about holding the hope of Clem's life in the palm of my hands.

"You should be getting along now," Gran says to Zoe.

Which is when the phone rings.

It's Si.

Si says we need to get to the hospital right now.

64

Zoe hugs me tight. "Good luck," she whispers.

But I don't think luck will have anything to do with it.

The journey to the hospital passes in a blur. A blur of colours. I cannot take my eyes from the flask; it swirls and changes continually. The closer we get to the hospital the more definite the new colours become. Peach, apricot, a flutter of pink. As we enter the hospital car park there isn't a single thread of green left. Not one. I don't know what it means, but the new colours are strong and warm and in that my courage holds.

We arrive, ascend the fifteen floors, and ring to gain admission. A nurse greets us, avoids eye contact, and leads us to a different ward in the Special Care Unit. I see Richie at once. There are a million wires going in and out of him, and ranged about him, overhanging him, are machines which hum and beep and flash. The bandages, which cover most of his tiny chest, disappear beneath his huge nappy. His fragility shocks me, if Richie is like this then Clem…

Clem.

Where is Clem?

Clem is not lying beside his brother in the cot.

He's not lying in an adjacent cot.

Clem is not there at all.

Without Clem beside him, Richie does not look whole, he looks like a ghost of himself.

"Poor little thing," says Gran in a whisper. "Oh, you poor little thing."

"Where's Clem?" I ask the nurse in a voice far too loud for this hushed and beeping place. "Where's my other brother?"

We cannot be too late. We cannot.

"This way," says the nurse, and we follow her through the ward to a side room.

Mum is sitting in a chair and Si is sitting on the edge of the bed beside her. Mum has Clem all bundled up in white in her arms. He's not hooked up to any machines and there's not a single tube or wire going in or out of him. This should be good news, but from Mum's face, I know it isn't. Mum isn't crying, but it looks as if she has been. It looks as if she has been crying all night.

The only part of Clem that isn't swaddled is his head. I'm close enough now to see his skin. It's not the right colour – it's a pale and slightly sweaty grey. Gran asks some question without moving her lips and Si shakes his head. But I already know why they've taken the tubes out of Clem and put him in Mum's arms.

They've put him there to die.

The hush in the room is suffocating, heavier than snow. The only thing holding Clem to the earth is his mother's love. Mum is holding that grey body as I imagine Aunt Edie once held Rob. Holding him so close you would have to kill her before she let go of him. And Si is so close to Mum he's part of it too, Mum is holding Clem and Si is holding Mum. They're all wrapped up there together in defiance of the whole world.

I take out the flask.

I don't know what I expect to happen, I haven't got that far. But this is what happens: nothing.

Nothing at all.

I wait and I wait and I wait and there's still nothing. No matter how I turn or hold or offer or clutch the flask.

I feel hopeless, sick, foolish.

Please, I say, I beg. *Please.*

No reply.

No reply at all.

It's as if death has taken our breath away and filled the room with stillness and silence and we're all just waiting and waiting for the terrible thing we know must come.

For minutes and minutes, there's nothing in this room but death, unless it's grief. That's one thing you can hear, grief, crying for itself like it did in 'For Rob'. I can hear all the notes and twists of it, sobbing and sobbing for the little boy who was never to grow up, whose life ended almost before it was begun. Edie's Rob. My Clem.

It's as if, somewhere very close, Aunt Edie is still playing the tune, her tune, 'For Rob', and weeping.

"No," I cry out. "No!"

Or maybe I don't cry out, because nobody hushes me, nobody does or says a thing. We're all in the same space and not in the same space. All locked together and apart. So I don't know, when the tune begins to change, whether it's me that's singing, or someone – something – else. Knowing what's inside and what's outside my head – I've never been very good at that.

But the 'For Rob' tune is changing; the minor chords, they're shifting slightly, just as they did in Aunt Edie's front room. It's coming, I think, it's coming, the creation song, only it isn't notes, it's more like a breath, or one of those very gentle summer breezes which carry sounds from somewhere so faraway you think you must be imagining it.

The breeze blows across Clem's forehead. There isn't much hair sticking out from under his white bonnet, but what there is quivers, one or two sandy strands of hair suddenly lifting, and despite the harsh hospital strip light above, sparking gold.

Hair of the lion.

My heart lifts, but Clem doesn't react at all.

Clem is still a closed-up little clam.

The breeze increases in intensity, blowing not just on Clem, but up my arms, raising goosebumps. Behind Mum the curtains begin to buffet and the sounds, such as they are, come closer. Get louder. More major, less sad. Gran said you can't smell a promise, so I don't suppose you can hear hopes and dreams. But that's what I think I'm hearing: hopes, dreams, and the sudden whisper of a woman.

Rob, Rob, I'm here.

She isn't here; my aunt isn't here. I'm not that stupid. But the hopes and dreams are. The hopes and dreams of anyone who brings new life to earth.

Which are my mother's dreams too as she hangs on, refuses to let go. Not now. Not ever.

Love can do that, I guess.

The song changes again, deepens and broadens, but it's nothing that I could ever play, nothing I could ever sing. No wonder I couldn't put my hands on it in Aunt Edie's house. It's way, way beyond anything I've ever heard before. Huge and strange and beautiful. I don't really know how to describe it, except to say this is how I think the earth would sound if you could hear dawn breaking or the roots of a giant redwood tree searching the soil for water, or the petals of a mesembryanthemum unfurling to welcome the sun.

Wake. Wake, my darling boy.

The words come on the breeze, tiny as a baby's snuffle, big as a storm wind. I cannot tell now which is stronger, the wind or the song, but the curtain behind Mum is flapping furiously. She moves her arm around Clem, perhaps to protect him, and that lets his head move, so he seems suddenly to be facing right into the wind. And all at once, he doesn't look so grey any more; there's a more natural glow to his skin, there's a peachy colour, a flutter of pink.

Of course – how could I not have known? Guessed?

I have to touch him, just to make sure. I have to feel what I can see, I have to touch the life that's coming back into his cheeks. So I reach and touch and all the noise subsides. The wind and the song both end the moment he opens his eyes.

He looks straight up at me.

And, of course, he's just a baby and babies can't focus, so actually he's not looking at me at all, he's looking through me, past me, to whatever lies beyond.

Then his little blanket lifts, as though he's taken a huge gulp of air and his ribcage has to rise as he breathes.

And breathes.

And breathes.

We all stare at Clem's chest, at its rise and fall. Rise and fall. And no one says a thing.

Except my stepfather.

Si, the Man of Science, says, "Oh my God."

65

Afterwards, we talk about what happened in that room.

Mum says, "It was a miracle. I told you those babies were miracles, didn't I? Right from the beginning, I knew. God's graciousness, His gifts to us."

Gran says, "I heard angels. Did anyone else hear that? It was like a choir, celestial music; I can't really describe it, voices faraway and yet terribly near, and so beautiful, it just made me want to cry."

And Si says, at first, "There was a strange sound in the room, not singing, I didn't hear singing, more like wind in trees, at the coast, where there's also the sea. And that curtain flapping madly as though there was some storm outside when there wasn't."

"A miracle," repeats Mum.

Si looks at her. "We have to be careful," he says.

"We're not out of the woods yet."

Mum looks at him. "Did you ever wonder why the babies chose to be born at Easter? At the time of spring and rebirth and Jesus?"

Si says, "Perhaps it was a mass hallucination."

"Stop," says Mum; "just stop."

And actually, he does. He stops.

It's not till I return home that anyone thinks to ask me what I saw or felt.

"What happened?" says Zoe. "What happened, what happened, what happened?"

"I heard the universe," I say, "whispering."

Zoe says, "No surprise there then."

It's wonderful to be able to tell her everything, every little detail. When I finish, she says, "You know that letter you wrote? The one you left on the doormat, about how your heart's all a mess?"

"Yes?"

"Well, it isn't. And you know what?"

"What?"

"Being your friend. It's just..." Zoe pauses, "... amazing."

66

Of course, the flask is empty. Though not empty in the sense of lonely or miserable, it's just empty in the sense of not being full. It remains iridescent, cool to the touch, beautiful. Not at all everyday – the flask could never be that.

I wonder what I should do with this marvellous empty flask?

I don't know, so it sits on my window sill like a piece of unfinished business. Also unfinished is the business of Aunt Edie's letter – and Gran. I want to talk to Gran about Rob, I want to know everything there is to know about the little boy who gave his life's breath to my brother.

"So why don't you just ask her?" says Zoe.

So simple. So Zoe.

I remember the look on Gran's face when she came into Aunt Edie's sitting room when I was playing 'For Rob'. That look, I now realise, was pain.

"I don't think I could," I say.

"Why?"

"I think it would hurt her."

"Why?" says Zoe again. "I mean, it didn't happen to her."

"I can't explain. I just feel, I feel I ought to... protect Gran."

"Your gran's an *adult*," Zoe says. She puts a big stress on *adult* as though if you were an adult you'd be beyond hurt. It's the first time I've ever really thought about adults hurting.

We leave it alone then, Zoe and I, but the letter doesn't leave me alone. It bangs about in my head. It's like it was with the twins: even when I'm not thinking about it I am thinking about it. About him. Rob. Aunt Edie's Rob. I mean, I didn't even know she was married.

I carry the letter around like I used to carry the flask. In my pocket. It bangs about in there.

Bang, bang, bang.

It's there when I come down for breakfast, or go to the park, or sleep. It's there when Gran drives me home from yet another visit to the hospital.

We're not out of the woods yet. That's what Si said, and it's true, though the doctors are surprised, in fact the doctors are amazed at the progress the twins are making. Especially Clem.

The drive back is rainswept, the windscreen wipers going so hard the outside world seems a blur and the inside world, the one that includes just Gran and me, appears very small and close. There's a box of tissues on the dashboard of the car, but when I want to blow my nose, I reach inside my pocket (the one that has the letter in) and pull out an old tissue. With the tissue comes the letter, I have it half in my hand and half not, so it spins a little and falls into my lap, the right way up. You can see the writing.

"What's that?" says Gran.

"A letter." Did I deliberately pull the letter into my lap? There doesn't seem anything up my nose that needs blowing.

"I can see it's a letter," says Gran.

"From Aunt Edie," I say. "To her son."

Gran nearly swerves into a Belisha beacon.

"What did you say?" asks Gran.

But I know she's heard. "I found it," I say. "In the bureau."

We are passing a lay-by; Gran brakes sharply and in we go. She yanks up the handbrake and turns off the car engine. Rain cascades down the front windscreen.

"Give it to me."

She takes the letter. I have it by heart, so I don't need to see the words to hear every one of them in my mind as Gran reads.

When she finishes, Gran doesn't say a word, just takes a tissue out of the box on the dashboard.

"I never even knew Aunt Edie was married," I begin.

Gran does blow her nose. "She wasn't. That was part of the problem."

"Problem?"

"Well, not *problem*. Look, it all happened a very long time ago and I'm sorry you found that letter. Such things are often best forgotten."

"I don't imagine Aunt Edie ever forgot," I say quietly.

"No," she says at length. "A mother doesn't forget a dead child."

It occurs to me she isn't thinking about Rob now, but about her own dead child, my father.

"What happened to him?" I ask. "To Rob?"

"He was stillborn. That's all. It happens. We never really got a proper explanation."

I can't help this random thought: if Si was telling this story, he'd know the details, he'd have done the statistics.

"We were pregnant together, Edie and me. A time of joy, despite everything." There's something softer in Gran's voice now, and further away, as though she's no longer sitting in a car in a lay-by in the pouring rain. "Edie just shone."

"She always shone," I say.

But Gran isn't listening to me.

"The man concerned, he was a musician, of course, an American jazz man on a tour of England, and he just swanned right on back to the States. But Edie didn't care – in fact, to be fair, I'm not even sure she told him. Edie only cared about the baby. Thought it might be her last chance." Gran pauses. "The babies were due within a week of each other. Rob on the 19th and your father on the 25th. Though your father was late, of course… Anyway, they would have been cousins, your father and Edie's Rob."

I imagine Gran holding newborn Dad in her arms and Edie holding an empty blanket. It makes my throat go tight.

"It must have been horrible," I say. "For Aunt Edie."

"And a blessing," says Gran sharply. "In a way. Those

weren't the days for having a child out of wedlock. And who knows how she would have coped financially. She was in cloud cuckoo land really."

I don't know about anything in or out of wedlock, or finances, or cloud cuckoo land, but I do know how I felt when Clem was grey and still. "Horrible," I whisper.

Gran clicks her teeth. "Well, you're right, of course. It was horrible for her. Especially seeing me and your father. And I never really understood that until…" She trails off.

"Until Dad died," I say.

"Yes," says Gran. "And even though your dad was hardly a baby, he was a grown man with a child of his own, but… well, I felt it then. The hole that a child leaves."

"She wrote that song, didn't she, in memory of him? 'For Rob'."

"Yes, she played it day after day, month after month. Drove us all mad with it. Drove me mad with it. I thought she needed to move on."

"It's strange," I say, and this, I realise, is partly what's been bothering me. "I always think of her as such a happy person."

"Well, she was, or was again – particularly after you

were born."

"Me?"

"Yes, you." And she starts the engine again. "You changed everything."

There seems something more to say, but Gran doesn't say it. She just drives hard and fast and in silence until she comes to the crossroads where it's right for her house and straight on for ours. She turns right.

"There's another letter," she says, "that you have to read, Jess."

67

As she unlocks her front door, Gran starts telling me that she would have given me the letter sooner, only there's been so much to do and the letter got muddled up with all sorts of other documents she cleared from the bureau and...

And she leads me through to her desk. The letter is not in view. In fact it's in a blue file inside a green file, in the very back compartment of a deep filing drawer. I would call it hidden.

"Here you are," says Gran, and she thrusts it into my hand.

For Jess, it says.

The writing is loopy blue, loopy blue ink.

For Jess.

My heart does a somersault.

This envelope is a long, white businesslike, one of the self-seal types where you can lift up the flap and then seal it down again to make it look as if you haven't read what's inside. And that's what I think has happened: Gran has read this letter already. But I can't really complain because I looked in *For Rob*, didn't I?

I pause long enough to wonder whether the contents of this letter addressed to me will have bang, bang, banged in Gran's brain like the contents of Rob's letter banged in mine?

"Go on," says Gran, impatient now. "Read it."

So I do, though it's difficult to see the writing because my hands are trembling.

My dear Jess, it says.

My dear Jess,

If you are reading this then I will be gone. But not quite gone, I hope. I hope when you go to the piano you will think of me sometimes.

It's impossible really for me to express the joy you've given me, ever since you were a tiny child. Ever since that first time I lifted you on to the piano stool beside me. I don't suppose you remember that day, do you? Well, most children that age crash and bang, but you put your tiny fingers down really carefully. You listened to every note you played. And every note I played too. I don't know how old you were then, not much more than three or four, I think. But I knew instantly.

It was like looking in a mirror. You too, I thought, are a maker of songs.

I don't know what you think, Jess, but I think there are connections between people. You aren't my child, you aren't my grandchild, but there's some bone of my bone that is your bone too. Blood of my blood. I couldn't love you more than if you'd sprung from my own body, my own soul.

Over the years you've given me so many gifts, I'd like to give you one in return. I want you to have my piano. I want you to play and play, so when I'm up in heaven (if they let me in!) I can look down and say: "There's my Jess." And they'll all say, "She plays better than the angels, doesn't she?"

With a very big kiss from your aunt,

Edie

I read this letter once, I read it twice, and I don't want to take my eyes off the paper because I can feel Gran looking at me, I can feel her staring me down, because she wants to know – as she always does – what my reaction is. I feel her all needy because Aunt Edie has said what we tried so hard never to say – bang, bang, bang – that we were always bits of each other. That we belonged.

Like Rob and Clem.

And I can see how this sits with Gran. It sits like me

trying to make a friendship bracelet for Zoe that also included Em.

Don't you understand best friends?

Don't you understand that a great-aunt cannot be as close as a gran? Nowhere near as close?

And that's why, I imagine, when Gran asked me what I wanted to have of Aunt Edie's and I said *the piano* her hand flew to her face as if I'd said *the moon*.

Bang, bang, bang.

But I know something about this feeling, a jealousy that stirs something deep, like when you think your best friend prefers beach ball Paddy to you, or like when you read two simple words.

For Rob.

Or perhaps *For Jess*.

I look up from the letter.

"Aunt Edie wants me to have the piano," I say.

"Yes," says Gran and waits.

And waits.

"Only our house isn't big enough, is it?" I say.

"No," says Gran, "it isn't." Her out breath is audible. "So you'll still need to come around to mine a lot, won't you?"

And I say, "Yes."

68

A week later, Si is back at work, I am back at school, and Mum is home more often. It's not exactly normal – the babies are still in hospital – but it's more normal than it has been.

On Saturday Si says, "Do you want to come out with me for a ride in Roger?"

The only difference between going out in an ordinary car and going out in Roger the Wreck is the noise. And the running commentary from Si on the wheezes and coughs and the perfectly fitting doors. And the fact that you don't really go anywhere. You just drive. Or he does. He just drives about.

"No, thanks," I say.

"It'll be the last time," Si says.

"What?"

"I'm going to sell Roger."

I get into the car.

I smell the familiar odours of leather and oil, polished wood, polished chrome, cold and dust. Si pulls out the choke and the engine spits into life. As we pull out of the driveway and into the road, I expect him to mention how quiet the engine is now that the timing chain's been fixed. But he doesn't. He doesn't say anything at all. He drives down the cul-de-sac and turns left and I don't ask where we're going because it doesn't matter. We roar up a hill to the screeching sound of the fan and we decelerate to the fut-fut noise of the exhaust and still Si says nothing.

So it's me who speaks first. "Are you going to get another car then?" I ask. "Now that Roger's running," I pause, "so perfectly?" I imagine a new car, a new wreck, just a bit of trim and half an engine in the garage and me being twenty-one by the time it's all fixed.

"No," says Si. "No one could replace Roger." He pats the walnut dashboard. "This little moggie. He's my first and last."

"Your last?"

"Don't look so surprised."

But I am surprised. I'm stunned. That would be like

me shutting the lid on the piano and saying, *That's the last time I'll ever play that then*, and expecting other people to believe me. Expecting to believe myself. And I realise I've never thought of this before, how this car is Si's piano, the place where he goes to be totally himself.

"But what are you going to…" I'm struggling for words, "… tinker with?"

Si laughs. "I think I'll be tinkering with the babies quite a lot. Or, at least they'll be tinkering with me."

The image of him spending his special moggie time with the babies makes me feel OK for him, more than this, it makes me feel warm inside.

"And – if I get any time left over from that," Si continues, "which I'm not expecting, I might start a veg patch."

"A veg patch!" I imagine it. Si digging the ground – having first read a gardening manual cover to cover. Si planting carrots in not-completely-straight lines. Si checking charts and adjusting the watering and the feed. The carrots growing into knobbly specimens of randomly different sizes. Si saying, "Look at these utterly perfect carrots."

Then I feel warm about Si himself. My stepfather.

"Have you told Mum?" I ask.

"What — about the babies or the veg patch?"

"About giving up the car?"

"Yes, of course. In fact, it was partly her idea. You see, the house is very small, as you know. But the garage…"

"Is huge," I say.

"Exactly. So we thought we'd convert it. Knock a window in the side, French doors, carpet. Make it into a playroom."

"A playroom?"

"Yes, for the boys."

And I know he's saying something he's never said before, never even dared think. He's saying the babies are going to come home. That they have a future, that they are going to grow big enough to need a playroom.

There's a gale-force wind coming through Roger's perfectly fitting doors and it's blowing at the hair on Si's head, and he's smiling and smiling.

"That's wonderful," I say.

And it is.

So how come my insides twist with jealousy?

Again.

69

The babies don't come home, not for weeks. Which is just as well, because that's how long it takes to clear the garage. The oily cardboard is folded up and thrown away, old tyre rims and engine bits that look like saucepans are advertised, spanners are rationalised, the old Britool box is put under the stairs and the Morris Authorised Dealer plaque with its picture of a red bull walking on black water is nailed up on the kitchen wall.

"Hang on," says Mum, "I don't remember saying that my kitchen was the new garage."

They almost have an argument about it, which actually I'm glad about because, for month and months, no one's had either the courage or the energy to have a row, so that makes things more normal too.

When you can almost see the garage walls again, men come and knock out a window and other men come with doors and sheets of glass. Concrete is laid and plaster skimmed.

And all the time, I look at the space. I look at just how much space there is in that playroom.

Zoe looks too. "Brilliant," she says, doing a cartwheel and a couple of backflips. "Perfect dance studio."

"Or grand-piano space," I say.

Of course I've told her the grand-piano story.

"So why don't you ask?" says Zoe. "Why don't you mention it?"

So simple. So Zoe.

I say nothing. It's all very clear to me now. Gran lost her only son. She doesn't want to lose her only grandchild. With the house getting busier, with the twins taking up so much of Mum and Si's time, what space will be left for old Gran? She needs me to have a reason to visit her, to be clamouring to visit.

"I'm not like you, Zoe. I'm not so good at saying things as you are."

Mum chooses green for the carpet. "Green's a very restful colour," she says. And then the walls go DH Linen White, which is actually a kind of cream. And finally, the weekend before the babies are due to come home, it's finished.

Si stands in the space and Mum stands in the space and I stand in the space.

"It's a beautiful room," says Mum. "I can just see them playing here."

I imagine the boys running up and down, playing football maybe, with a squashy patchwork ball.

"Yes," says Si. "And I can see you playing here too, Jess."

"What?"

"I can see you…"

"We can see you," says Mum.

"Playing here," they say together.

There's a rumble in the driveway, as if the biggest moggie in the world was reversing over the gravel. Outside the French doors is a removal van.

"Surprise," says Mum.

I can't help my hand flying to my mouth, like my mouth was a little moon.

Because, of course, it is a surprise and yet I know at once what it is.

Two men get out of the removal van and press some buttons and the back door scrolls and clatters upwards.

Revealed, brass feet first, is the grand piano.

Aunt Edie's beautiful, beautiful grand piano.

Its lid is down and it's all tied up to keep it secure.

"Gran told us," says Mum, "about Aunt Edie's letter."

And suddenly Gran is here too, parking in the cul-de-sac. She must have followed the removal van, so as to be here at this moment when the men are throwing the blankets off the piano and preparing the trolley.

It's hardly any time at all before they swivel the piano and prepare it to come down the ramp, as though it was earth's most majestic creature emerging from Noah's Ark after the flood.

They have to put boards on the gravel, to stop the piano sinking in, and they have to put boards up to the French doors too. Everyone is talking at once.

The men are saying (through puffs and heaves), "A little to the left, Rod. I said left." And, "Mind that window, Dan. Dan!" And it reminds me of the time when the men puffed upstairs with the bureau. A time that seems both yesterday and a million years ago.

Mum says, "Gosh, it looks a little larger now it's actually here," and Si says: "Of course, it will need retuning; I'm not sure pianos like being moved that much," and Gran says, "Edie got one sent out to India once."

I say nothing at all, I just watch this huge, shining piano coming into my home.

Aunt Edie's piano.

My piano.

Gran says, "Are you pleased?" She grabs me by the arm. "Are you pleased?"

"It's a gift," I say.

"Yes," says Gran flatly. "From Edie."

"And also from you."

"Me?"

"Yes." Because I know what it's cost her. "Thank you so much, Gran." Hugging her I realise I'm about half an inch taller than her and will probably get taller still. "Do you know what this means?"

"What?" she says.

"If you want to hear me play now, you'll have to come around to my house."

"You think?" she says.

"Yes. And as I'll be playing a lot, you'll have to come round a lot, won't you?"

I might be wrong, but I think there's a tear in those tough, dry eyes.

70

It's a school day when the twins finally come home.

"Can I come and see them?" says Zoe. "Can I, can I, can I?"

Of course, I say yes, although Zoe, being Zoe, would have bounded in anyway.

The space in the hall that used to be the perfect place for the Tinkerbell upright piano, is now perfect for a double buggy. All the equipment in our house is double, including the Moses baskets on their double rocker in the playroom.

"When they get bigger," says Mum, greeting me, greeting Zoe, "they'll have a basket each, although they'll rock together. You see how one push moves both baskets? But for now…"

For now, the babies are small enough still to be side

by side, lying together on some floaty blue mattress surrounded by floaty white blankets. They look like they dropped straight from heaven and are still clutching little bits of sky and cloud.

Zoe looks in the basket. Both boys are fast asleep, their lips wobbling with dreams. "Oh," she exclaims. "Oh, look at them. They're so cute, so gorgeous, so... scrunchy."

"Scrunchy?"

"Yumptious. Yummy. I could eat them up."

"You could?" I peer in the basket. I try to see my brothers as Zoe sees them, and for the first time, they don't fill me with fear. There they are in their basket, quite ordinary.

"Yes," I say, "they're adorable."

"Couple of pests," says Mum. "That's what they are. You don't have to get up in the night for them." But she's smiling like she just invented the universe.

"Can I come and see them often?" says Zoe.

"Of course," says Mum.

"I'll help them build bricks."

Mum laughs. "Not for a bit."

"And I'll dance for them too. And in a few years, when you and Si and Jess want to go out, I could babysit them."

"We'll see," says Mum.

I like the fact that Zoe has my brothers in her future, it helps me believe they are really here to stay. I'm glad she sees me in her future too, the two of us together. Friends. The idea that I was all for hating her, refusing to speak to her, chopping her out of my life – that all seems very strange to me now. But then perhaps you can't really love a person unless you can hate them too, that it's the flip side of the same coin. I mean, nobody hates an acquaintance, do they? You have to feel powerfully about someone to be able to hate them.

"When are they going to wake up?" says Zoe.

"Not for a bit," says Mum. "They've only just gone down."

"Oh," says Zoe, all disappointment.

"You'll have to come back another time."

"Can I?" says Zoe. "Can I come back tomorrow and the day after that and the day after that?"

"You'll get bored," says Mum.

"No, I won't."

She will, of course, but Mum just smiles and I smile too.

When Zoe leaves, Mum and I sit quietly in the playroom with the sleeping babies. The late-afternoon sun pours through the French doors. After a while

Mum says, "What are you thinking, Jess?"

As it happens, I'm thinking two things simultaneously. I'm thinking how Em will come and visit the babies and Alice too, and maybe even Paddy. And then the visiting will stop, and we'll know they really are here to stay. Clem. Richie. Nothing to remark upon. I'm also thinking about love and hate. How I hated Si when he said he was my parent and he wasn't, and how I loved him when he mended the timing chain so the babies wouldn't die, and so maybe it is right that you can't love someone without being able to hate them too. I try to explain the hate thing to Mum.

"Only with you," I tell Mum, "it doesn't work, because I've never hated you."

Mum laughs that very gentle, beautiful laugh she has.

"Plenty of time yet," she says. "You probably just need to get a little older."

"But I don't want to hate you!"

"And I don't want you to hate me. The point is only that you have the option; you can. You can feel safe to." She pauses. "Sometimes, when a child loses a parent, rowing with the only parent they have left feels dangerous."

"So you mean if I had a row with you, I'd be being brave?"

"Yes. Exactly."

"I'll think about it," I say.

"But then you're brave anyway," says Mum. "Brave and very special. But I think I've said that before."

"Not about brave," I say.

Mum smiles. "Speaking of which, it all looks fine with Zoe now?"

"Yes. Closer than we were before, I think."

"That's how it goes," says Mum. "It's only when you're on the point of losing something – someone – that you really know what you've got."

"That's not what you said last time."

"Oh?"

"You said we might be growing out of each other."

"I offered it as a possibility, that's all. That it's OK to move on sometimes."

"And also OK to stay together. To make it work."

"Yes, of course."

"You know what, Mum?"

"What?"

"Sometimes I think, Zoe and me, we might grow old together, be on our Zimmer frames together. Live next door to each other maybe, like Gran and Aunt Edie."

"So long as you don't bicker like they did."

"Well, maybe we will."

"Yes," says Mum. "Maybe you will."

The front door opens. Si is home, but I haven't finished with this conversation yet.

"What's a soul, Mum?" I ask, not quite out of the blue.

"Mmm?" says Mum. She's listening to Si, the noise he makes in the hall with his keys and a drawer. "Sole fish, sole shoe, soul as in not-body?"

"Soul as in not-body."

"Well, your spirit, I guess. Your essential spirit." Mum looks in her sons' basket. "The colour with which your life burns."

Iridescent pearl and fizz-heart summer sky blue and moonlit white and lion-mane gold and new-shoot green and fluttering pink and even howling black.

"Is that what you meant?" asks Mum.

I don't have a chance to reply before Si comes in.

He's obviously overheard us talking because (as he looks in at the twins and gives Mum a peck on the cheek) he says, "Not what the Romans would have said. Anima – that's the word they had for the soul. Not so

317

much colour as wind or breath. Did you know that?"

"No," says Mum.

"I did," I say. Strong as a storm wind, tiny as a baby's breath.

"Oh," says Si. "That school of yours must be doing a better job than I thought."

71

Si goes upstairs to change out of his suit. I keep looking at the babies, expecting them to wake.

"Babies always sleep longer than you think," says Mum. "Sleep, feed, excrete, sleep. That's pretty much it for babies."

"But I want them to be awake," I say. "I want to play a song for them."

"Well, play away. They'll hear it in their dreams. Your aunt Edie always said that – people respond to music even when they're asleep."

"I never heard Aunt Edie say that."

"You weren't the only person Edie spoke to, you know, Jess." Mum gets up. "Suppose I better start thinking about making some food for the rest of us."

As she heads for the kitchen, I draw the rocking

Moses baskets closer to the piano. I want to be able to see the babies' faces as I play.

"This is 'Spring Garden'," I announce. "One of Aunt Edie's favourite pieces. This is the grass growing. Can you hear the grass, Richie? And this bit's the cherry trees, bursting into bloom. Can you hear the blossom? And the birds, singing in the tree? Can you hear the birds, Clem? Are you dreaming birds?"

I lean over the baskets. Clem is not dreaming anything, Richie is still fast asleep, but his brother is awake. Clem is wide awake.

"Oh, Clem, do you like it? Do you?"

No reply.

Bit like the flask.

"I'll teach you. I'll teach you everything I know. Everything Aunt Edie taught me. Would you like that?"

No reply.

But he's listening, he's listening to the music and also to the sound of my voice.

"You'll be good," I say. "You'll be a brilliant player, you know that?"

No reply. He's staring at the ceiling.

"Better than me, I reckon, because of your beautiful soul. You owe that to Rob you know, Edie's Rob. You got to be really lucky there, Clem."

A little munching sound of his lips.

"You're scrunchy, Clem. You really are. Why don't you chat back?"

Clem scrunches and munches.

"I love you," I hear myself say before I realise that Mum is standing in the doorway.

"Has he woken up?" she asks.

How does Mum know that?

"I think he's going to be a better player than me," I say. "Clem. Better at the piano. Better at songs."

"Oh, I don't know about that," says Mum.

But I do. I know it like Mum knows that Clem has woken up even though she wasn't in the room and he never made a sound. I imagine all the family standing around Clem when he's nine or ten, or thirteen or fourteen. I imagine them saying, *Where did all this boy's music come from?*

And Si saying, "It can't have been from my family."

And Mum saying, "Nor mine for that matter."

And me saying, "It came from Aunt Edie."

And both of them laughing and saying that although Edie was my aunt, she wasn't Clem's aunt; she's only a relation through my father, so it can't be that.

Which is where they're going to be wrong.

"Maybe it was you," Mum might add. "Maybe it's you that has helped Clem get where he is?"

And that will be wrong too, but not wholly wrong.

72

Aunt Edie's house is sold.

"To the couple you met," says Gran. "The ones that looked around the house the day of the twins' op."

"I'm glad," I say. "I liked them."

"Yes," says Gran. "So did I. She's pregnant apparently, so there'll be a baby in the house soon."

"And she plays the piano," I say.

"Oh, how do you know that?"

"She talked about it, or her husband did."

If we buy this house I will always remember you and your music.

"Do you want to go around one more time?" asks Gran. "Say goodbye to the house and all that?"

"No," I say, perhaps too fast. "Thank you." Without Edie, without the piano, the house is, well, it's like the flask. Empty.

"Fair enough," says Gran.

"There is one thing I would like though," I say. "As I'm here."

"What's that, Jess?"

"A sprig of eucalyptus."

Gran doesn't ask why I want a sprig from her eucalyptus tree, she just goes to the kitchen drawer and gets out her secateurs.

"Come on then."

We go to the gate between the houses, which is bolted shut, and stand by the eucalyptus tree.

"Do you want to do it yourself?"

"Yes, please."

"Remember to cut it at an angle, and just above a leaf stem. It's better for the plant that way."

I cut a small piece, only five or six leaves long.

"That's not much," says Gran.

"It's enough," I say.

"I think I'll take some too," says Gran, and she cuts herself a number of small silvery branches and then adds some orange trumpet daffodils from the border.

She offers me daffs too, but I say no.

"Sure?"

"Sure."

"Suit yourself."

She arranges her flowers and then soaks some kitchen roll in water to wrap around my single eucalyptus stem.

"That should keep it moist till you get back home."

"Thanks, Gran."

"Do you know what eucalyptus means, Jess?"

"I didn't know it meant anything."

"Most plants are supposed to have some sort of properties. Eucalyptus is usually associated with protection. And healing."

When I get my little piece of healing home, Mum says, "Do you need a vase for that, Jess?"

But I've already got one.

Because this is what I have decided to make of my marvellous empty flask. I fill the flask from the tap in the bathroom, and when the water gets up to the neck, there's a sudden rush of bubbles so, just for a moment, it looks like there are little seed fish. Swimming.

I don't know how or why, but the bubbles keep on coming long after I put in the eucalyptus stem, some of them rise to the surface of the water and burst, but others, millions of others, cling to the inside of the glass like stars in a tiny galaxy. I stand the flask on my bedroom window sill, put it in the exact spot where the breath used to sit and wait. Late-spring sunshine slants in dead straight lines through the windowpane, but the mountainous whorls and the impurities of the glass – and the bubbles – tease and refract that light so my little flask shines and shimmers, just as I hoped it would.

And of course my stem of eucalyptus will die, because everything that lives dies, I have learnt that. When that happens, I'll go out into the garden or into the wood behind the park and I'll find something new: a leaf, a blade of grass, a bluebell, a nettle perhaps. In high summer, I might ask Mum for a rose. A pink rose in bud with brown papery petals outside. Because everyday things are made anew, I've learnt that too. The vase will hold all of these treasures and every time one falls away, another will rise.

So there will be a rhythm to the flowers and a rhythm to my remembering. And when Clem's old enough, maybe I'll tell him about Rob and the flask and how there are always things in the universe bigger than your understanding.

But then again, when I look in his fizz-heart blue eyes, I think he may know that already.

Acknowledgements

Very grateful thanks to Dr John Young, a Morris Minor enthusiast who allowed me access to his little moggie called – um, Roger the Wreck. Any resemblance between his Roger the Wreck and mine is purely coincidental. Gratitude too to Ron and Innes, my local garage men who have not just kept my old banger running for the best part of twenty years but who will also, if you slip them the odd doughnut, tell you about crankshafts and timing chains. Any errors are obviously mine.

My thanks to the Brighton Buddhist Centre and to Padmavajri (Lotus Diamond Thunderbolt) in particular, for her time and her generosity. Thanks also to Naissa Essart Nielsen – aged 11 – for her swiftly delivered and candid thoughts.

And then there's Peter Tabern. Peter was the first person to notice that Jess was a girl. It's a long story… which he read on several different occasions in several different incarnations, each time holding up a lantern so I could see what I'd actually written. Thank you very much, Peter. Every writer needs a Peter Tabern, but they don't all get as lucky as me.

There's also Charles Boyle. He didn't allow me to thank him for what he did on my last book (*Knight Crew*) because he published it and he's ludicrously modest. But he's not in charge of this book, so here are the thanks, belated but very sincere. Tough luck, Charles, you can't win them all.

Last but not least is Rachel Denwood. She decided she wanted to be my new editor before she'd seen a word of *The Flask*. It's this sort of faith that keeps a writer going.

Also by Nicky Singer

essentialmodernclassics

Feather
Boy

NICKY SINGER

"A book that engages the mind and touches the heart."
David Almond